Other Than a Halo

VALERIE COMER

GreenWords Media

Dedication

If you struggle to believe
God has not only forgiven your sin
but forgotten it,
this book is for you.

Acknowledgments

I can't tell you how much fun it was to visit Helena, Montana, again! It had been two and a half years since I'd written *More Than a Tiara*, and something — Bren Haddock — kept pulling me back to that story world. She needed her own happy ending, but the story didn't begin falling in place until I realized that Rob Santoro, casually mentioned several times in *Secrets of Sunbeams* from the Urban Farm Fresh Romance series, would be perfect for her. What a joy it has been to write Bren and Rob's story as well as set the stage for the third Christmas in Montana Romance, *Better Than a Crown* (2017), featuring Heather Francis.

I'm thankful to my friend Angela Breidenbach, Mrs. Montana 2009 and co-author with me of *Snowflake Tiara* (2014), who coached me in the ways of pageantry. Even though she had much less input into *Other Than a Halo*, I'll always value her friendship, the emails, the long Skype calls, and the visit we made to Helena together.

May I simply say thank you to my readers and fans? You all are awesome! I love to hear from you when something in the story touches your heart.

I'm thankful to my street team for their daily encouragement, and to my beta readers: in this case, Elizabeth Maddrey, Melanie Pike, and Debbie Jamieson. Thank you for helping me to make this story stronger.

A big thank you to my fabulous editor, Nicole, who sees beyond words, punctuation, and sentence structure to the heart of the story.

I'm also grateful for the Christian Indie Authors Facebook group and my sister bloggers at Inspy Romance. These folks make a difference in my life every single day. I'm thrilled to walk beside them as we tell stories for Jesus!

Thanks to my family: my sweet husband, our kids and their spouses, and our grandgirls. I'm so blessed!

Thank You, Jesus, for the promise in 2 Corinthians 5:17 (ESV): Therefore, if anyone is in Christ, he is a new creation. The old has passed away; behold, the new has come.

Books by Valerie Comer

Farm Fresh Romance Novels

Raspberries and Vinegar
Wild Mint Tea
Sweetened with Honey
Dandelions for Dinner
Plum Upside Down
Berry on Top

Riverbend Romance Novellas

Secretly Yours
Pinky Promise
Sweet Serenade
Team Bride
Merry Kisses

Urban Farm Fresh Romance Novels

Secrets of Sunbeams
Butterflies on Breezes
Memories of Mist

Christmas in Montana Romance Series

More Than a Tiara
Other Than a Halo

Chapter 1

"Don't you think it would be great fun for both girls?" Bren Haddock stared at the mother of her daughter's best friend. "Um, no. I pretty much think you're crazy."

"What's crazy about it?" Kristen O'Brien's brown eyes lit up with excitement. "It's not competitive like the Miss Snowflake is for adult women. It's just for fun."

Bren spun her pottery mug on the table in Helena's Fire Tower Coffee Shop and raised her eyebrows. "Have you never heard of Crowns for Kids?"

"Of course I have." Kristen giggled. "Wasn't that *reality*—" she air-quoted the word "—show nuts? There was nothing real about it. And this won't be anything like it."

Bren had watched several episodes, aghast at what some people would do for fortune and fame. She shook her head. "I can't believe you want to put Lila and Charlotte through that. No way."

"Todd and I will gladly pay Lila's entrance fee and buy her dress—"

"No. I'm not a charity case."

Kristen's eyes softened. "I know that, Bren. I know how hard you've worked to get on your feet and make a solid home for your kids all on your own. How hard you work every single day. This is something Todd and I want to do. Call it our Christmas gift to Lila. She'll have a couple of adorable outfits and some happy memories of a perfect Christmas week spent with her bestest friend in the whole world." Kristen's voice mimicked Lila's.

"I don't see how it can lead to anything good." Bren met her friend's eyes across the wooden table. Around them, the lunch crowd drifted out. "I really don't. I appreciate that you guys have money and run in different circles than we do, but I don't want to get dragged into this. I don't want Lila thinking she can have whatever Charlotte has. She needs to learn to be satisfied with what I can provide, not want what other people have."

"I—"

"Being a single mom is hard, Kristen. I didn't even graduate from high school, thanks to being pregnant with Davy."

Kristen's hand touched Bren's arm. "I'm sorry you had to go through all that. I really am. I know you don't regret Davy and Lila, though."

"You're right. I love my kids, but look at me. I'm twenty-six with a nine-year-old and a seven-year-old. I finally got my GED and am taking college courses via correspondence. I'll be fifty before I get my degree at this rate. I want better for my kids."

"The pageant can help."

Bren shook her head. "Back to that, are we?"

"I'm serious. It will help teach both girls poise. Remind them there are hopes and dreams to reach for. And there are scholarships." Kristen leaned closer. "Besides, Marisa will coach them. You know how much they both adore her."

Who would ever have guessed that being one of the former model's projects would lead to all this? On a couple of underused acres and in her spare time — hard to believe her friend had any of that — Marisa and her mother had invited several single moms to grow food for their families.

Bren chose her words carefully. "Marisa is amazing. I can't thank her and Wendy enough for teaching me to cook and preserve food. I'm not the only person whose life she changed in more ways than one. She introduced me to Jesus." She chuckled. "But her year as Miss Snowflake isn't over until Christmas Eve, plus she's marrying your brother in January. How could she possibly have time to coach the girls?"

Also, why on earth were they still having this discussion? Did that mean Bren's resolve was weakening? Surely not.

"How about if their pageant dresses were their flower girl dresses?" Kristen's eyes sparkled. "How about if their talent was a song they could perform at the wedding?"

Bren sipped her now-cold coffee. One more try. She tilted her cup toward her friend. "Kristen. Look. I'm a black coffee kind of girl. No frills. I can't even remember what yours is called. I appreciate your friendship. I really do. But we're not in the same league."

"It's a sugar-free, white-chocolate mocha with a shot of peppermint and no whip." Kristen laughed. "And our taste in caffeine has nothing to do with life." Her gaze went past Bren's head. "Oooh. There's someone I want you to meet." She waved frantically then beckoned.

Bren turned slightly in her chair.

A tall guy with dark curly hair lifted his hand in response as he walked toward the front counter.

She swiveled back and glared at her friend. "Kristen. Don't even start."

"Start what?" Kristen winked. "He works for Todd at the ad agency. A Christian and new to Helena. What's not to like?"

The man placed his order at the counter, giving Bren the chance to look him over. Those curls brushed the collar of a tailored suede jacket that ended at narrow hips. He glanced over his shoulder and met her gaze. A small smile played at the corners of his mouth.

Bren snapped her gaze back to Kristen.

"Cute, isn't he?" whispered her friend. Her traitorous friend.

"Looks that way." Bren kept her voice even. "I really should get going. I have to—"

"School isn't out for another hour. You don't have to be anywhere."

"Kristen."

"Hmm?"

"Stop trying to set me up. I'm not looking for a man, okay?" Even good-looking guys could be jerks. She should know.

"It's not like tha—" Kristen glanced over her shoulder. "Oh, hi, Rob. Care to join us?"

He towered over the table, a mug in his hand. "Hello, Kristen. Nice to see you. I don't believe I've met your friend." His dark eyes looked Bren over.

Bren's lips tightened into a hard line.

"Rob, this is Bren Haddock. She's the single mom of Charlotte's best friend, Lila."

Way to slide in the single part.

"Bren, this is Rob Santoro. He recently moved here from... Spokane, wasn't it, Rob?"

He nodded as he flipped a chair around and straddled it. "Via Billings. But yes, I'm Spokane born and bred. Most of my extended family still lives there, all within about six blocks of each other."

"But you escaped to Montana." Kristen giggled.

Rob's grin was lopsided. "Someone had to. Big families have their place, but I got tired of everyone being in my business all the time."

"I wouldn't know." Kristen sighed. "When my parents bought Grizzly Gulch Resort a few years ago and my little brother moved here to open his photography studio, it didn't take Todd and me long to decide Helena trumped Salt Lake City. We love being near family."

15

"My father has four brothers. I have fifteen cousins. They all live in Spokane. Every last one of them except for a couple who escaped for college. They'll be back."

Bren could only imagine. Much as she craved a sense of family, Rob's did sound a bit overwhelming.

"How about you?" Rob turned to Bren. "Do you come from a big family?"

"No." No need to tell a guy she just met that her parents' bitter divorce had estranged her from both of them. "It's just me and my kids."

Kristen placed her hand on Bren's arm. "My parents have all but adopted them, though. And the church has, too. Everyone needs family."

It was hard to let down her guard. Bren had been on her own for so long it still seemed hard to believe she'd found any sort of security. One of these days the rug would get pulled from under her, and she'd be on her own again. Granted, she had more skills than before and a bit of savings now, but where could a high school dropout whose job experience was farm operation find another job? Marisa and her mom both said Bren could keep managing and living on Hiller Farm, but someday that would change.

"Todd says your specialty is marketing for events. Bren and I were just talking about the Miss Snowflake pageant for the little girls. Todd says you'll be the one handling that?"

Rob glanced at Bren, questions in his eyes.

She raised her chin. So she didn't look the part of a pageant mom. What did it matter? She'd turned Kristen down. What this guy thought of her didn't make a speck of difference.

Why did that seem like a loaded question? Kristen looked innocent enough, but Rob had been to the O'Brien house for dinner a couple of times, and he knew she had a quick wit with complex thought processes. He'd bet anything she was matchmaking, but what man wanted a ready-made family? Not him. Still, he wouldn't be rude. Couldn't be.

"Yes, Todd asked me to handle that portfolio." He smiled at Bren. She was pretty in an earthy way, with wavy blond hair pulled into a long ponytail. He turned back to Kristen. "If you have any ideas for the marketing campaign, I'm all ears. I'll admit I've never done a promo for a pageant before, and I'm still debating what angle to take with it."

"There are two stages. I think. The first is awareness and getting people to sign their daughters up for it. And then, once we have a full complement, marketing to get viewers interested. That part will be easier because the events will be in tandem with this year's Miss Snowflake events."

Bren shifted in her seat and glanced at her watch.

Kristen touched Bren's arm. "Don't rush off. You still have plenty of time before Lila and Davy's bus."

Bren pushed back her chair and glared at her friend. "I'm not sure why I'm in this discussion, as we won't be taking part. I can catch up with you later."

"Bren. Please."

"Kristen. No."

Rob looked from one to the other. Interesting. Todd had laughed, saying his wife was a force to be reckoned with. The evidence was in front of him as she stared down her friend, not giving an inch.

Bren sighed. "This conversation is over, Kristen. I don't see any need to parade Lila around in makeup, slinky clothes, and overdone hair, pretending to be on a manhunt. She's seven. Just a little kid who should be allowed to be one."

"What part of *this is not Crowns for Kids* did you miss? It's a no-glitz pageant. I don't want Charlotte acting seventeen either."

"It's the gateway drug. Don't you see?"

Rob checked his own watch. Did he really need to listen to them hash it out?

Kristen turned to him. "This is where the first stage of marketing comes in. Many of the parents will be just like Bren: concerned about pressuring their little girls to grow up too quickly."

Bren crossed her arms. "This is a bad thing how?"

"Of course," Kristen went on, "there will also be little divas signed up who already demand their wishes on a silver platter. That can't be helped, but we will stand firm and create a family-friendly atmosphere."

Rob was beginning to see the challenge. Bren had fire in her eyes. No pushover, this one. She likely had to be strong to raise her kids alone. "Bren, I'm interested in what your objections are. You mentioned not wanting your daughter to grow up too quickly. Can you fill me in on some of the other issues you see?"

Kristen hid her smirk behind her coffee cup.

Bren glared at her friend before turning to Rob. "That's the big one, but money is another." She held up a hand as Kristen opened her mouth to speak. "I don't know how much it costs, but just the fact that Kristen offered to pay for it tells me it's outside my budget. There's clothes she'd need, coaching, hair and makeup—"

"I told you. No glitz."

Rob pulled out a notebook and began scribbling.

"—driving her to practices and events. Keeping family life balanced with Davy. And most of all, raising her hopes that she'll win and then her being crushed. Fairy tale meets crash ending right at Christmas. Talk about timing."

He finished his shorthand notes and glanced up. "Anything else?"

She leveled him a stare. "I think that about covers it."

Rob chewed on the end of his pen. "Maybe her dad would be willing to help with expenses." Although what if Bren were widowed, not divorced? Had he put his foot in it?

Her chair scraped on the wooden floor as she surged to her feet. She set both hands on the table and leaned in on him. "Maybe he's in jail for dealing drugs. Maybe he's out again. I've lost track. He's never been interested in

Lila, and I'm certainly not going to remind him. I'd prefer he kept on forgetting."

Bren's brown eyes glittered in her almost elfin face. Rob felt himself staring, caught up in her firestorm.

"I *am* leaving now. Nice to meet you, Rob. I'll deal with you later, Kristen." She grabbed a bright green oversized purse held together with buckles and strode toward the door, skinny jeans tucked into calf-length boots.

Kristen giggled. "Well, I think that went over rather well."

The door jingled shut. Bren's brown jacket crossed the window then disappeared.

Rob forced his gaze back to his boss's still chuckling wife. Kristen might not be wrong.

Chapter 2

"Mommy, Charlotte says she's going to be Miss Snowflake like her Aunt Marisa."

Bren closed her eyes and leaned over the kitchen sink. "She is, is she?"

"She says she is getting a pretty dress and playing a song on the piano in front of lots of people. She says it will be fun."

"That's nice for her." All Bren could think about was getting even with Kristen. "She might not win, though. In pageants, a lot of girls compete, and only one is the winner." They wouldn't talk about runners-up.

"Charlotte says…"

"You know you don't get to do everything that Charlotte does, right?" Bren glanced over her shoulder.

"I know." Lila slumped at the table, shoving mini marshmallows beneath the hot chocolate with a spoon. "Is it because she has a dad?"

Bren's heart clenched. "Partly. Plus, her mommy and daddy have more money than I do."

"But we have a nice big house to live in now instead of the apartment. I don't have to share a room with Davy anymore."

"I know, sweetie. But it's not because Mommy is rich. It's because I work for Marisa and Mrs. Delaney. They needed someone to live in this nice house now that Marisa's mom married Mr. Delaney."

Lila nodded. "And take care of the farm."

"Yes. And that."

"But why can't I be Little Miss Snowflake, Mommy? Why can't I have a pretty new dress and sing a song?" Lila's brown eyes peered up at Bren from behind long lashes damp with tears. "Charlotte says that is my talent. Want to hear?"

"It's okay, sweetie. I know you can sing really well." Gah. Would it be so terrible to accept Kristen's offer? A side benefit might be seeing Rob Santoro again. That would be worth something, too.

No, it wouldn't. She was tough. She couldn't trust herself to find a good man, not after the mistakes she'd made in the past. If she'd ever had a halo, it had long since disintegrated from tarnish and corrosion.

A man like Rob Santoro wouldn't be looking for a woman like her, if he were even looking at all. Which he probably wasn't. Just like *she* wasn't. Then why hadn't she been able to get his dark curly hair, deep eyes, and broad shoulders out of her mind since Kristen had introduced them a few days ago?

"When is it Halloween, Mommy? Me and Charlotte want to go trick or treating. Can I be an angel?"

Bren pressed a kiss to her daughter's blond head. "You are always an angel, sweetie. Don't ever forget it."

"But I want to be one for Halloween." Tears welled up in Lila's eyes again.

"We're going to the party at Grizzly Gulch Resort." Good grief. Had Bren ever been as needy as this child? She hadn't dared to be. Her mother would have cuffed her upside the head and told her to get over herself. Her dad would have done worse. Bren took a deep breath. She'd protect these kids with everything in her, but could she be overprotective?

Davy slammed in the back door, Baxter on his heels. "Mom, there aren't hardly any eggs today." He scooted the egg basket onto the counter and rubbed his hands together. "It's cold out there."

The dog flopped onto the mat in the corner of the kitchen, nose between his paws as he watched them.

Bren glanced out the window at the gray sky. She'd tasted the tang of incoming snow earlier. "Winter will soon be here."

Her son's face brightened. "Winter means tobogganing down the hill and snowball fights."

"And snow angels," said Lila.

Davy rolled his eyes. "You're such a girl."

"She *is* one, bucko. Be nice."

"Sorry, Lila."

He wasn't. Not really. Some days it was hard enough to figure out how to mother a girlie girl who longed for pretty things, but it wasn't any easier trying to be both parents to a rough-and-tumble boy.

Maybe Kristen was right. Maybe Bren should consider marriage.

In her mind's eye, Rob Santoro's eyebrows rose over chocolate-colored eyes.

Or maybe she'd been right the first time. No guy in his right mind would want to be saddled with her and her two kids.

~~~

Todd O'Brien stopped in Rob's office doorway. "Kristen said she'd talked to you about the portfolio for the Little Miss Pageant. Have you given any thought to the angle?"

Rob lifted his gaze from his computer monitor. "Some." Not as much thought as he'd given Kristen's gorgeous friend, something he wouldn't admit to his boss.

"Do you have any ideas?"

Besides that her hair looked amazingly soft? "Uh… I'm afraid you might have to sell me on the pageant myself. I'm okay with grown women putting themselves through it, but why push a little kid? Kristen's friend — what was her name…?"

"Bren?" The look on Todd's face told Rob he wasn't fooled by the apparent forgetfulness.

"Right. Bren. She said she didn't think it was a good idea for little kids, and I can see her point. I realize this is my job, but how can I market this event if I suspect it's a bad idea in the first place? It's easier to sell Montana tourism to the world. It's such a great place, there's no hesitation. No dark side."

"I understand what you're saying. I can order you to do it, but I suspect your campaign will be more effective if you put some heart and soul into it, not just a fear over losing your job." Todd waited until Rob's gaze met his before continuing. "Your job isn't on the line, by the way. This isn't the sort of thing I'd fire a guy for."

"Good to know." Rob chuckled, feeling the relief. He hadn't realized there'd been anxiety of this very thing deep inside until Todd's words.

"But still, I'd really appreciate it if you could come up with some kind of publicity campaign. It's more Kristen's thing than mine, but I think the girls will have a lot of fun. It's way low key compared to an adult pageant. No glitz. No fake hair. No sexy clothes or dance moves. Those will get a girl automatically disqualified, so I don't think it will be a problem. Any parents who spend this much are going to obey the rules."

Rob thought of Bren's mention of money. That couldn't be easy for a single mom. No wonder she didn't want her daughter to participate.

"If it goes well this Christmas, we will likely add more age groups next year. Back in the 1800s when the first pageant was held, the purpose was to remind the world that Montana has a lot to offer. Even though we're not in Europe or back east doesn't mean we can't pull off culture and sophistication."

Rob nodded. "Got it. I'll have something on your desk by Monday."

"You did great on the Halloween promo, by the way. My in-laws are pleased with how many families have signed up for the party at Grizzly Gulch Resort Friday night. You're coming, aren't you?"

"Uh, I hadn't planned to." How long had it been since he'd gone to a Halloween party? Not since he was a little kid growing up in Bridgeview and Nonna had all her grandkids over, plus the other half of the neighborhood.

"Why just sit at home when you can come out to the inn and meet people? My parents have all kinds of things planned. You don't want to miss it."

Rob quirked a grin. "I'm accustomed to spending Friday nights at home alone, to be honest. It's not an issue."

"No way, man. Kristen would never forgive me, and neither would her mom. Say you'll come at least for an hour or two. We start at five with a hot dog roast out at the fire pit."

Is this where he said he avoided processed meat and junk food like the plague?

"They're not cheap mass-produced wieners, Santoro. Not for my in-laws."

"I happen to know what they're charging a head for this event, so I'd hope not. I did all the promo, remember?"

Todd laughed. "Just say you'll come. Schmooze a bit. Get to know some folks from the church and the neighborhood."

Would Bren be there? Rob couldn't help but be curious what her kids would be like. What kind of mother she'd be.

Knowing Kristen, she wouldn't take no for an answer from her friend any more than Todd would from Rob. He heaved a deep sigh. "Fine. I'll come."

⁛ ⸙ ⸙

"You're bringing a case of apples from the market, right?"

Bren shifted the phone to her other ear. "Yes, it's on my list."

"And the pumpkins for the carving contest."

"Yes, Kristen. We've gone over the list like a dozen times. No need to panic. I don't think I've ever given you reason to believe I'm unreliable."

"No, of course. I'm just nervous."

"It's a kids' Halloween party. What's to worry about?"

The silence went a few heartbeats too long. "Nothing, really."

"Kristen."

"Okay, so there are a few families coming that I hope will sign their little girls up for the pageant. I just want to make a good impression on them. Let them know the girls will be in good hands."

Bren should have figured. "Families like mine."

"Oh, not you. You already said no. I won't nag you."

That'd be a first. Nagging wasn't the only way Kristen O'Brien got her way. Bren would need to be on the lookout. "Fine. Look, if I'm going to have everything ready on time, I should get back at it. Thanks for inviting Lila straight off the bus. She was pretty excited."

"No problem. Those two are no trouble when they're together. Besides, they wanted to try on their costumes ahead of time."

A niggle wormed its way through Bren's mind. "What's to try on? I thought their angel costumes were pretty basic. Two of Todd's old white shirts on backwards with a glittery belt and headband."

Kristen tittered, sounding nervous. "Until my mother got hold of the idea and ran with it."

Bren stopped in the middle of her kitchen. That niggle turned into a heart attack. "What do you mean?"

"Oh, no biggie. She just ordered the girls' costumes online. They'll be so cute."

"Kristen O'Brien. We've talked about this sort of thing. Recently, in fact."

"I know. I get it, really I do. Only I forgot to tell my mother."

"And then you forgot to tell me."

"Yeah. Sorry. You're not mad, are you?"

Bren took in a deep breath and let it out as she silently counted to ten. "Leave a girl with some pride intact, would you?"

"The Bible says pride is a sin."

"Kristen."

Her friend heaved a big sigh. "I know. I'm sorry."

"Okay. Whatever." By the time on the clock, Lila had probably already seen the fancy new costume. How mean would Bren seem, ripping it away from her and throwing it at Ruth Mackie? She couldn't do it. But she really needed to find some friends who wouldn't push her around like Kristen.

How could she stay angry, though? Kristen was the real thing. She was just a bit overenthusiastic about integrating Bren and the kids into their family's life. Bren could only be thankful that Davy was older than the girls, while Kristen and Todd's son, Liam, was younger. At least she didn't have to deal with both kids' heads being filled with all this nonsense way out of their reach.

"Look, I really need to go. I hear Davy coming down the stairs now."

"Oh, one more thing?"

Those words filled Bren's heart with dread. "What? Make it quick."

"Rob Santoro is coming."

"Rob who?" Bren forced her voice to sound confused, even though the image of the hot man sprang to mind with no hesitation.

"You remember. He came into the Fire Tower the other day when we were there. He works for Todd."

"Oh, right. I remember now. What about him?"

"He's coming tonight. Really, Bren. Don't you listen to a word I say?"

"Nope. Not if I can help it. See you soon." Bren hung up and chuckled. It might not keep Kristen at bay, but it was the best she could do on short notice.

Chapter 3

I've heard so much about you, Rob." Jase Mackie gave Rob's hand a firm shake. "My brother-in-law speaks highly of your work."

"Good to meet you, too, Jase."

Dozens of people roamed the parklike grounds of Grizzly Gulch Resort. A bonfire lit the center of the area, while strings of solar lights created enough lighting for the remaining yard. Food tables had been set up in the gazebo under soft lighting. Rob had to admit the Mackies threw a good family party.

"Todd tells me you're creating the ad campaign for the pageant. If you need any specific photos, let me know, and I'll see what I can do."

Rob nodded at the other man thoughtfully. "I could use some images of local children already entered. Not that

31

there are many. We plan to launch the campaign just before Thanksgiving."

"How about before and after photos?"

"Oh, that would be great. Although Kristen said it was a no-glitz pageant."

Jase laughed. "There's still a big difference between little girls in jeans and T-shirts and ones wearing pretty dresses with their hair in ribbons."

"I imagine so." Rob's older sister had never been a tomboy, but some of his girl cousins sure had been. He'd seen the difference when they put in an effort.

A woman came up beside Jase and slid her arm around him. He bent to kiss her before turning back to Rob. "I'd like you to meet my fiancée, Marisa. Marisa, this is Rob Santoro, Todd's new hire."

This was the City of Helena's famous Snowflake Queen? Rob could believe it. She was gorgeous even in jeans and a polar fleece jacket. He reached toward her. "Pleased to meet you."

"Likewise." Marisa smiled and shook his hand. "Jase, have you seen Bren? Kristen said she's here somewhere, but I can't spot her."

Arms around each other, they turned and scanned the yard. Jase pointed. "Is that her over by the apple-eating contest talking to your stepdad?"

Rob pulled his gaze away from the pair. It had been a long time since he'd given much thought to a woman in his life, but lately he'd begun to notice the couples around him. Was it time to find someone special and settle down? His grandmother would say long past time. Rob's lips curved into a rueful smile as he thought of her relentless matchmaking, one of the many reasons he'd left Spokane several years before.

That was definitely Bren beyond the bonfire. She'd pulled her hair into a long braid tonight. She chatted with an older man several inches shorter than herself while tying apples to a line stretched between two trees. As he watched, she tossed back her head and laughed. Was it his imagination, or could he hear it way over here above the chatter of the crowd?

Bren was real. He'd liked that about her when they'd met at the coffee shop, too. She wasn't trying to make an impression on anyone. If she was on the hunt, it didn't come across. It had been Todd's wife who seemed to try to set them up.

Would being set up be all that bad?

If it wasn't at Nonna's hand, maybe, but Kristen O'Brien seemed to use similar tactics. First an introduction, then constantly looking for ways to throw them together. Although to give credit where credit was due, no one had shoved Bren at Rob in the twenty minutes since he arrived.

"Hey, have you met Bren Haddock?" asked Jase.

At least, until now. Rob braced himself as he refocused on the man he'd been talking to. The man whose fiancée was strolling around the bonfire, and Rob hadn't even noticed her leaving. "Uh, yeah. Your sister introduced us the other day."

"She's a good friend of both Kristen and Marisa. Single mom."

A wave of irritation sloshed over Rob. "So I heard. What were you saying about the pageant promo?"

"I'm doing some preliminary shooting for the official booklet this next week. My niece, Charlotte, will be one of the contestants, so I can get you some photos."

"Sure, sounds good." Ideas began to percolate.

"Kristen's working on Bren, so maybe her daughter will be there, too."

The annoyance increased. "Bren didn't sound very interested in the pageant the day I ran into them at Fire Tower."

Jase shrugged. "She'll come around. It's a good deal for her, and the little girls have their hearts set on it."

"Why don't you guys back off and let her decide for herself?

"Whoa." Jase met Rob's eyes. "No one's making Bren do anything. Not that we could, even if we wanted to."

"It sure sounds like everyone's mind is made up of what's best for her." Just like in his family. If working for Todd O'Brien was going to remind him of growing up Santoro every time he turned around, he should never have taken the job and moved to Helena. He hated pressure. Manipulation.

Maybe he shouldn't have made a career of marketing, either. Always trying to convince people they wanted something they didn't know they needed. Whatever. He loved his job. Really. It was watching his friends blindside Bren Haddock that he didn't like.

Across the bonfire, Marisa and Bren hugged. Bren talked, waving her hands, then threw back her head and laughed. This time Rob was sure he heard it.

"Obviously Lila won't compete if Bren doesn't sign her up."

A quick glance at the other man showed he was watching the women, too. Jase had more of an excuse than Rob did, as he was engaged to one of them.

Jase turned back to Rob with a grin. "Lila's a natural drama queen, though. I honestly think she'll have a blast in the pageant. But, whatever. Let me know in the next few days what you'd like to see from the shoot, and we'll go from there. I'm sure it doesn't matter to you who's in the photos."

As of a few minutes ago, Rob did care, but he wasn't going to announce it. "Will do."

⌒⸌⸜

"Okay, are you kids ready?"

Five eager little girls eyed the apples dangling above them.

"One, two, three, go!"

Bren couldn't help laughing as Lila and the others tried to catch the apples in their teeth. Instead, the fruit rolled around their heads while they giggled. This could take a while. Long enough to glance around and see where Rob Santoro was now. She'd seen him talking to Jase a while back, then over by the pumpkin-carving station, but she'd lost track of him after that.

Not that she had any real reason to watch him. It's just that he was one of the few people here she didn't know, and that made him intriguing. That's all it was. The other adults were people she knew from church, fellow growers from the Tomah Community Supported Agriculture, or parents of her kids' friends. Rob was the only person who didn't fit into a tidy slot.

"Eeek!" Charlotte squealed.

She'd managed a tiny bite of her apple and was now having trouble catching the same spot.

"I haven't seen some of these fall party games since I was a kid."

Bren jumped at the low male voice behind her. "Oh, you startled me."

Rob chuckled. "I didn't mean to. I was wondering if you'd had a chance to get a hot dog."

"No, not yet. Marisa said she'd be back in a few minutes to watch the line here. Then I'll see what else is going on."

"It's quite the party. Do the Mackies always do it up so big?"

"Seems like it." Bren clapped as Lila got a bite out of her apple. "Good going! Catch it again!"

"Reminds me of when I was a kid in Bridgeview. I haven't seen a pumpkin carving contest for years, and I'm not sure what all is going on for the older kids."

"I'm not sure, either. Kristen is the organizer. I try hard not to know too many things, because the more I know, the more she ropes me into."

His dark eyes crinkled at the corners when he grinned. "Ever heard of saying no?"

"You haven't met Kristen." She heaved a sigh. "Okay, you have. So you might have an idea why the association is so dangerous."

"Does that mean you're signing your daughter up for the pageant?"

Bren wiped the grin off her face. "Are you kidding me? That's Lila in the middle of this group."

Rob angled his head and looked at her daughter.

What did he see? The same thing Bren did? Lila's wild hair didn't look like it had been brushed in a week. She had dirt smeared on her jeans, and her jacket had tattered cuffs. All that plus what looked like applesauce on her cheek.

"Cute kid." Rob shot Bren a smile. "Jase was saying he was doing some before and after photo shoots. Any of those girls would be a good candidate for the befores tonight."

Bren laughed. She couldn't help it. Charlotte O'Brien looked just as bad as Lila. Little girls were meant to play and get dirt on them, not primp in front of audiences.

Rob joined her in laughter, a deep, rolling sound that warmed her to her toes. Just because Kristen had maneuvered them into meeting didn't mean he wasn't a nice guy. Just because he'd sought her out tonight didn't mean he was looking for a relationship. He probably didn't know that many people in Helena yet and could use a friend. And she always had room for one more.

"Way to go, Charlotte!" came Marisa's voice from behind her.

Bren turned.

"Go get something to eat," Marisa said. "Hey, Rob, have you had a hot dog yet?"

Okay, so it wasn't just Kristen. Fighting them all was too much effort. She was an adult and allowed to have male friends. Kristen and Marisa couldn't make her fall for Rob, or make him have feelings for her.

"I was headed over there when I got sidetracked by apples." Rob's grin took in both of them. "I might have to challenge Jase and Todd to this contest after a bit."

"Oh, you're on," Marisa said quickly. "I can hardly wait to see you guys with your hands tied behind your backs trying to catch an apple."

Bren chuckled. "Ditto. It's definitely not the fast way to eat. I think Lila's gotten three bites in the last ten minutes."

Rob's eyes gleamed. "Of course, if the guys do it, you gals should, too. Fair's fair."

"Oh, I don't think so—" began Marisa.

"Sure, why not?" Bren raised her chin and looked at Rob. "Or we could string them all at the same time and have a race."

He quirked an eyebrow. "You must have done this many times if you think you can take me on and win."

"A few." She raised her eyebrows right back at him. "I'm willing to take the chance. I've lost before and lived through it."

"In that case, we'll do it."

"But..." The sound from Marisa was rather weak.

Rob held his bent arm to Bren. "Let's go get a hot dog and some of that hot potato salad I smelled when I passed the gazebo."

She couldn't resist but tucked her hand behind his elbow. "Sounds like a plan. We'll be back with the others in a little while, Marisa. Be sure to save half a dozen apples."

They moved off a little way from the apple line before Rob glanced back and chuckled. "I don't think she knows what hit her. You sure you're up for it? Because you know I can't let you back out now."

Bren started to remove her hand, but his arm tightened against his side, trapping it. She looked up at him, suddenly aware of his touch.

He looked down at her, eyes widening slightly as though he was thinking the same thing.

Uh oh. No doubt others were watching. Marisa, for sure. Probably Kristen, too. Bren pulled her hand away firmly and offered him a rueful grin. "No need to give them anything to talk about." Then her face heated. What if he hadn't caught the vibes from the others? What if he thought she was making it all up? Oh, man. Just what she needed.

Rob winked. "I suppose you're right."

He placed his hand on the small of her back and steered her around a group of older kids doing a bean bag toss.

Bren picked up speed, but Rob stayed right with her, his hand warm and steady. No, this couldn't be happening.

How could she remain so aware of that one small point of contact? It was one thing for Kristen to have a harebrained idea and quite another for Bren's emotions to go along with it.

Kristen's dad, William Mackie, came over the sound system in a booming voice. "If you're entering the costume parade, you've got fifteen minutes to prepare and come to the back of the stage."

Bren turned, looking for Lila, but Marisa waved her away from across the yard. Fine. She'd let Marisa and Kristen deal with the girls. She still hadn't seen the angel costume Ruth Mackie had ordered without asking.

Was it so bad allowing people to do things for her and the kids? They weren't doing it to chalk up points but because they were friends. They even knew all about her past and loved her anyway. A guy like Rob Santoro, though... he wouldn't stick around. Still, hadn't he heard what she said about Lila's dad? Maybe he already had enough information to avoid her if he was going to.

She looked up at him, and he grinned down. "What do you want on your hot dog? Looks like German night at the resort. I'm seeing sauerkraut for the dogs as well as hot potato salad. I didn't realize I was so hungry."

Bren shoved aside her misgivings. "The Mackies' chef is excellent. I'm hungry, too. Then I need to find a good spot to watch the parade."

"Let's do it." He nudged her into the gazebo.

Even Ruth Mackie's wide-eyed smile as she looked between them from behind the serving table wasn't enough to make Bren tell him no.

Chapter 4

"Hey, can I give you a hand?"

Bren jumped and yanked the jack out of her phone. "Don't sneak up on me, Marisa! You about gave me a heart attack."

Her friend grinned. "Sorry. I could hear the music from outside the greenhouse. You're going to kill your eardrums at that volume."

"Yeah, yeah. I know. I just needed it loud enough to keep me focused." Bren looked around the greenhouse with its scrubbed planting tables and sighed. "Running a commercial garden is a lot of work."

Marisa grimaced. "Don't remind me. You've done most of it for the last year. I really appreciate it. I hope we're paying you enough."

Marisa and her mom had entered Hiller Farm into the Tomah Community Supported Agriculture program several years back, offering residents of Helena more options in their weekly boxes of organic food. The situation had changed when Marisa won the Miss Snowflake Pageant last Christmas Eve. Her schedule of appearances kept her hopping all over the US, working to make healthy food available for children, leaving most of the farm management and labor to Bren and a few volunteers.

"My life is so much better than before the kids and I moved out to the farm, I can't even begin to tell you how grateful I am for this opportunity."

Marisa sighed. "That doesn't answer my question."

"I didn't hear a question." Bren grinned. "You and your mom have provided a new beginning for me and the kids. Have you decided how hands-on you want to be next year? You won't be traveling as much, I assume."

"That's the thing. I won't be traveling for pageantry, but Jase has some contracts for documentaries overseas, and I'd like to go along. Habitat for Humanity is one. I've kept in touch with Heather Francis from last year's pageant. Do you remember her? She works for Habitat and hooked Jase up with the directors."

Bren nodded slowly. "So you need me to stay on."

"Do you want to? You may have made other plans by now, while we were dithering. Of course, Mom has also talked about selling the farm. She has her hands full with Bob's place."

No one had seen Marisa's widowed mother's romance coming last year, but she'd married the CSA's founder on Valentine's Day and moved out to the Delaney Farm a few miles down the road, leaving space for Bren and the kids in the Hiller farmhouse.

"I can't afford to buy it."

"I know. I told Mom that we should leave things alone for now, unless you wanted out."

Bren grimaced. "I hate to be the one keeping your mom tied to the farm. If you want to sell, go ahead. The kids and I will land on our feet." Somehow.

Marisa rested her manicured hand on Bren's stained sleeve. Yeah, like that. Bren could be thankful at the unlikely friendship and opportunity, but she wasn't in the Hiller or O'Brien league. Her heart sank a little further. Or the Santoro league, no matter how Rob's attention had flattered her the other evening.

"Bren. That's not how it is. You've done a terrific job here. Mom doesn't need the money from selling the farm anytime soon. Neither do I. Jase just moved into our new house near the resort. There's absolutely no reason for us to yank your home and job away from you. All we ask is that you let us know as far in advance as possible if you change your mind so we can make plans."

"Huh. You sure?" How could anyone have so much money that the funds from a farm like this wouldn't be welcome? "I can't see me doing anything else for a lot of years. At least as long as the kids are home." She didn't even want to think about being alone when they grew up, but in ten years Davy would be gone and Lila a high school senior. She shoved the thought to the back of her mind.

"Perfect, then. Mom and I will draw up a contract sometime soon. An agreement we can all review and sign annually to formalize the verbal agreement we had this year."

Hopefully it wouldn't contain any nasty surprises. Bren gave herself a mental cuff to the head. When had Marisa or Wendy ever treated her unfairly? They hadn't. They'd gone above and beyond to make sure she had everything she needed, right down to a new laptop and enrollment in an online college so she could begin working toward a horticulture degree.

"Okay. Sounds good." Impulsively, Bren reached out and hugged Marisa. "I thank God for you every day."

Marisa hugged her back. "And I thank Him for you. You are an answer to my prayers in so many ways. A genuine friend."

Bren shook her head. "I'm still not too sure about all that."

"I know you're not. But that doesn't keep it from being true. I know people have let you down in the past." Marisa's brown eyes shone in sympathy. "And I can't guarantee Mom or I will never add to that. We're human. But you can depend on God. He will always meet your needs. Always."

"Thanks." Bren blinked back tears.

"So, one more thing."

"Yes?"

"About the pageant. I'd like to pay Lila's entry fee and other costs."

Bren grimaced. "Get in line. Kristen—"

"Yeah, she told me. Is it because you don't feel like you deserve it?"

"Um."

"Bren. You're the daughter of the King. A princess, remember? He's redeemed you. You are just as worthy as any woman in Christ. And Lila is just as deserving as any other little girl to get dressed up, be pampered, sing a song, and have some fun."

The war inside Bren was real. She knew those things. She did. But...

"If you then, who are evil, know how to give good gifts to your children, how much more will your Father who is in heaven give good things to those who ask Him?" Marisa quoted gently. "Jesus' own words in the book of Matthew. He doesn't want you to cringe in the shadows, sweetie. He wants you to reach out for His good gifts."

"Are you telling me the pageant is *God's* gift?" That might have sounded sarcastic, but Bren wasn't used to being soft. Wasn't used to handouts. She'd earned everything in her life through sheer grit.

For by grace you have been saved through faith. And this is not your own doing; it is the gift of God, not a result of works, so that no one may boast. The words from Ephesians two trickled into Bren's mind. Okay, she hadn't earned salvation. It was a freely offered gift with no strings attached.

"It might be. For sure it's a gift from me. Will you accept it?"

Bren met Marisa's gaze. "You drive a hard bargain."

"I haven't even started." A grin twitched Marisa's cheek.

"No glitz? No glam?"

"Promise."

"Fine then." And it had nothing to do with seeing Rob Santoro.

Nothing at all.

⌒ ⌒

Rob sat at the back of Jase's photography studio with his laptop open, working while he waited for the photoshoot to begin. Pretending, anyway. He'd tried not to notice — not to care about — Jase's list, but Lila Haddock's name had all but leaped off the screen in between Emily Abercrombie's and Charlotte O'Brien's.

Bren had said yes to Kristen.

He wasn't sure what to make of that. What to make of the whole assignment, really. How could pageantry for kids be a good thing? He didn't have to agree. He could ask Todd to handle this event himself or hire someone else to do it. Rob wouldn't get fired over it, but he didn't object strongly enough to test Todd's promise. Honestly, he was more curious than anything. Pageantry was a world away from any assignment he'd taken on before.

The door opened and three chattering little girls entered, dressed in jeans and jackets. Four women followed them in, but Rob's gaze caught on Bren. She looked amazing today. How could she be different, though? She was wearing the same jeans, the same jacket, the same boots.

She glanced his way and gave him a tentative smile. Her hair was looped in a messy bun at the back of her head. And she was wearing makeup. Not a lot, but there was definitely a blush to her cheeks that hadn't been there last time he'd seen her in daytime. Her blue eyes popped, and her lips glowed.

Maybe he recognized it because of the gel he'd added to his own hair before he left the apartment this morning.

Rob couldn't help the slow grin that spread across his face. Had she really done all that for him? Unless Jase had promised the moms a moment in front of the camera, he couldn't think of any other reason. He gave her a nod.

Bren flushed and turned to Marisa, Kristen, and the other woman, who must be Mrs. Abercrombie.

Kristen glanced his way. "Where's Todd?"

"In his office. He said it was my portfolio, and he didn't need to be here. Said I could boss Jase around."

She shook her head. "Guess I'll have to stop by the office afterward then."

"If you have something for him, I can drop it by."

Kristen laughed and wiggled her eyebrows. "I'll deliver my own kisses, thanks."

Aw, man, how could he have guessed? "Probably a good idea."

Marisa dropped a kiss on Jase's lips as the others hurried into the room off the studio. Then, to Rob's surprise, she came and stood beside his chair.

"First up, we have Emily Abercrombie. She's got some attitude I'm hoping Jase will capture in the shots. As far as she's concerned, she's already won."

Rob scrolled to the appropriate heading on his laptop. "A bit of a diva, then." He glanced up as the mother and daughter re-entered the room.

Marisa nodded. "There's one in every crowd. If she's the worst we get, I'll count it all good." She strode to the front and gave Emily instructions.

The child struck a pose in front of the white backdrop. Then another. After several dozen rapid clicks, Marisa asked Emily for her sweetest smile. The transformation was immediate. Rob would never have guessed this winsome child would ever give any sass.

"Good job, Emily!" Marisa gave the child a hug and turned to her mother. "Saturday's shoot is outdoors over at the playground. Casual play clothes, everyday hair. Kind of like she looks when she gets home from a busy day playing with a friend."

"I'm not sure the before photos are a good idea..."

"Oh, they are." Marisa offered a brilliant smile. "You'll need to trust me on this. It's part of the package for allowing Emily to participate in the pre-event marketing."

"If you're sure."

"I insist."

48

Priscilla Abercrombie still looked doubtful, but she nodded and beckoned to her daughter. "Time to go, baby."

Kristen and Charlotte came out next. Marisa and Jase led his niece through the poses as well.

Rob made a few notes, thinking of how he could use the photos in his campaign. Mostly, though, he waited for the final pair.

Lila erupted from the prep room with dramatic gestures.

"Good job, Lila! Now let's see your hands on your hips. Look thoughtfully up into that far corner." Marisa talked her through the remaining poses.

Rob tried to pay attention, but Marisa's voice faded as he watched Bren leaning against the doorjamb, watching her daughter.

Was he going to do something about this? Ask Bren out, maybe? What was appropriate when dating a single mom? Some kind of family activity?

She probably wouldn't agree.

Just then, she turned slightly, and her gaze collided with his.

Maybe she would, after all.

But it was rather a big commitment, even to take the first step. Her life was very different from his. Two kids, and from what she and Kristen said, by two different men. He pondered that while holding her gaze. Did it matter that she wasn't a virgin?

At least he didn't have to wonder. He knew.

Rob tried to imagine taking Bren to meet his family in Spokane. Now that would be the litmus test. Mom and Dad would be thrilled he'd found a Christian woman and be thankful for two more grandchildren. Francesca would want to be Bren's new best friend. His young niece and nephew would be delighted to have cousins. Well, Tieri would, anyway. Luca was too young to care. Nonna would demand to know if Bren had even a dribble of Italian blood.

Just the thought brought a grin to Rob's face.

Bren smiled back.

Yeah, one more step.

Chapter 5

Bren waved goodbye to Davy and Lila as they mounted the school bus steps at the end of the driveway. Then she bolted back into the house, trembling as she surveyed her makeup tray. Four times in one week? Some kind of record.

Why bother? The first couple of times Rob had seen her au naturel and he'd still taken a second look. But she was pretty sure nature could be improved upon.

Breakfast date. Who'd ever heard of such a thing? The challenge had been finding a time when she didn't need childcare. Rob said he'd earned the right to be late for work this once. That likely meant Todd knew.

Bren peered in the mirror as she swirled mascara on her lashes. Too much? Aargh! She didn't know. She'd been out of the dating game for years and had expected to keep it that way.

Until Rob.

It hadn't been love at first sight, but there'd been a definite attraction.

She plucked an errant hair from her eyebrow.

Rob Santoro is interested in me.

She'd replayed those words a million times since Saturday's photo shoot. At the end, he'd asked her if he could take her out, and they'd agreed on Tuesday breakfast. This was either the start of something fantastic or the stupidest thing she'd ever done.

Bren smoothed down the front of the lacy emerald green top she'd found in a consignment store a few months back. She'd never worn it, because *hello*? Where to?

Her hair. Should she put it up? She bunched it and mounded it on her head. No, that was silly. It was breakfast. Not a night at the Helena Symphony. *Breakfast.*

A glance at her watch made her heart stutter even faster. He'd be here any minute.

Rob Santoro.

She'd be seen in public with a good-looking man. A really good-looking man. Okay, hot. In public. People would see. Wonder.

She should cancel.

It was too late to cancel.

Downstairs, the doorbell rang, and Baxter gave a low woof.

Bren was out of time. One last look in the mirror to straighten her necklace, and she headed down the staircase to the front door.

Rob stood on the step in jeans and his suede jacket. The corners of his eyes crinkled as he smiled at her. "Good morning. You look amazing."

Her? He was just being polite. But why would he pretend?

She straightened and smiled back at him. "Come on in for a minute. I'll just get my jacket and boots on."

Baxter's wet nose touched her hand.

"Hey, nicelooking pooch." Rob crouched just inside and gave Baxter's ears a scratch.

"He's a good boy. Really he belongs to Marisa's mom, but she left him with me when she married Bob Delaney last February. Bob has several farm dogs, and they decided it would be easier on this old guy to stay in his familiar place."

Rob gave Baxter a final pat and stood. "This isn't your farm?"

Bren zipped up one boot. "No, I'm the onsite manager for Marisa and her mom, Wendy. Hiller Farm is part of a CSA, and it's my job to keep everything running smoothly."

"Wow, that's cool." Rob took the coat she was reaching for and held it as she slipped it on.

"Thanks." She picked up her purse. "Ready to go."

He held the door of his SUV as she slid into the leather interior. It was nice. Newish, but not too intimidating. She dared breathe.

Rob started the vehicle down the highway toward town. "How did you come to be a farm manager? I'm not even sure what degree that would require."

Even to herself, Bren's chuckle sounded nervous. "None at all. Wendy offered me the job with no training other than what I'd already picked up gardening with them for two years. I'm taking distance ed right now, but it will be years before I have a degree at this rate."

"Good for you, being so dedicated."

He didn't know the half of it, but he might as well know if it was going to make him run. "I didn't even finish high school, Rob. I was pregnant with Davy. I went from one bad relationship to another until Lila was four years old. Then Marisa started a program for single moms here in Helena, giving us garden space, teaching us how to grow food and then cook it. Even how to preserve it. It was through her I saw Jesus' love in action and became a Christian."

She glanced over at Rob as they pulled up in front of Steve's Café. Looking for the rejection she was sure to see. "I'm no angel, Rob. I'm not a great catch by anyone's standards."

He put the vehicle in Park and turned to face her. "You're a great catch by God's standards."

Bren blinked. "Well, yes. He's not as picky as everyone else. I'm thankful for it."

"You know that God doesn't categorize sin. We've all disobeyed Him. We all need salvation."

"I know, but..." Bren snapped her mouth shut. They'd have a nice meal, hopefully, and then she probably wouldn't hear from him again. But at least he knew up front. He couldn't pretend he hadn't known.

His hand touched hers. "Ready for breakfast?"

Bren met his warm gaze. No sympathy. No condemnation. Nothing different than before. She smiled back at him. "Ready."

$\backsim$ $\subset$ c

Rob couldn't remember the last first date he'd had when he'd laughed so much. When he'd felt so relaxed in a woman's presence. When he could hardly wait to do it again.

Even now, watching Bren's animated face across the table at Steve's, he couldn't help grinning.

"—and Davy couldn't figure out why trying to teach a Lab to retrieve eggs from the chicken house might be such a bad idea. He'd heard so much about their gentle mouths he was sure it was one chore he could pass along."

"I had a Lab mix when I was a kid." Rob hadn't thought of her for ages. "She was a great companion when I got tired of hanging out with all the cousins."

"But you lived in the city. It must have been tough for a big dog like that."

Rob shrugged. "Bridgeview is down along the river. There was plenty of wild space there. Still is, though they've cleaned it up some and made a park out of part of it."

"Wild?" She quirked an eyebrow at him.

"Yes, wild." He winked. "Coyotes and deer and bears kind of wild. They come in along the river. Not so great to have that interface close to downtown, but there haven't been too many serious problems. Everyone knows not to leave their garbage out and that gardens need tall fences around them."

"Sounds like a pretty nice place."

Rob thought back. "It was. Is. I like Helena, though. It's smaller than Billings, plus it's enough closer to Spokane that I can pop back for a weekend if I want."

"It must be nice to have a family." She poked at the remains of her huckleberry-stuffed French toast.

"It is. But when a quarter of your neighbors are your relatives, it makes a guy a bit claustrophobic. Everyone is constantly in everyone else's business, and my nonna is the worst of all. 'Let me introduce you to a nice girl, Roberto. She's Italian. You will like her.'"

"Nonna?"

"Grandmother. My dad's mom is practically the Queen Mum of Bridgeview." He shook his head. "No one else ever calls me Roberto. Just Nonna."

"I guess your grandmother wouldn't like me. I'm not Italian." Bren's eyes widened as her cheeks flushed. "Not that it matters. I mean..."

Rob covered her hand with his. "I think she'd like you." He held her gaze as long as she'd let him.

"I doubt it," she said to her almost empty plate. "I'm pretty sure no one's grandmother thinks a wreck of a single mom is perfect for the family."

"Bren."

She peered at him through lowered lashes. "It's only the truth."

Much as he didn't want to, he heard and understood her words. "I think *wreck* is too strong a word. I can't begin to imagine what your life has been like. What brought you to this moment in time. But I can tell you one thing." He waited until she glanced up at him again. "You have a lot of inner strength. You're a good mom. You have loyal friends. You have a job with a lot of responsibility, and you're doing it without the benefit of a degree or diploma. How does the word *wreck* fit into all that?"

Bren pulled her hand out from under his. "I don't know. It's just what I am." She glanced at her watch. "Wow, I really need to get going. Besides, doesn't Todd expect you to show up yet this morning?"

Against his will, his eyes found the clock across the restaurant. He hated it, but she was right. Todd wouldn't hassle him, but the breakfast crowd had drifted out and office workers on coffee break had started to arrive.

As soon as Bren stood, he surged to his feet and held her jacket for her. He stuck a few bills to cover the meal and the tip into the folder the waitress had left half an hour ago and shrugged into his own jacket before following her out the door.

"Thanks for breakfast." She poked her toe at a crack in the sidewalk.

"My pleasure. We'll have to do it again."

Bren shot him a surprised look.

"Or maybe something with Davy and Lila. Anything you guys like to do that I could join you in?"

"Are you serious?"

"Yes." Rob stood a few feet away from her, hands in his pockets. "Why wouldn't I be?"

She waved a hand at the restaurant. Through the window he caught a glimpse of the waitress clearing off their table. "Didn't you hear a word I said in there?"

"Bren. The same goes for you. Weren't you listening?" He didn't dare touch her for fear she would take it wrong, but he needed to get through to her. Why it was so important, he didn't know.

She took a deep breath and let it out slowly. "I heard you. I just didn't think you meant it."

Rob held her gaze as steadily as he could. "I'm not in the habit of lying." Still, he somehow felt at the edge of a cliff, ready to jump off, hoping his chute would open. Bren was not someone he could date casually. Her self-esteem was a mess. Even one date seemed to carry a whole lot more pressure than he'd guessed. Another one, with or without her children, would either make her push away completely or practically render them engaged.

He'd been avoiding a committed relationship his entire adult life. Did he have what it took to follow through to the end? Did he even want to?

She blinked. "I'm sorry. That's not what I meant."

His brain scrambled to connect the dots and remember what she was referring to. "I'll give you a ride back to the farm while you think about what we could do Saturday. Unless you already have plans?" The least he could do was give her an out.

Bren allowed him to tuck her into his SUV, and remained silent as he drove out past the city limits.

His hands clenched on the steering wheel. "Bren? I don't mean to push you. If you're not interested — if you don't want to see me again, please say so."

"I just... just can't believe I didn't scare you off." Her voice held a tinge of wonder.

Rob flashed her a grin. "Not afraid. Intrigued, but not afraid."

"Oh. Well, that's good, I guess. Um, Davy has been wanting to go to Exploration Works. It's kind of a science museum for kids over on Carousel Way." She looked away. "I haven't had a chance to take them."

"That sounds interesting. What time should I pick you up? We could go out for lunch, too. Or supper, if you'd rather go later in the day." He turned into the farm driveway with gardens on either side. A greenhouse and garden shed took up part of the right hand side, and the house with its wide veranda sat straight ahead. Everything looked well kept. Cared for. That had to be Bren's doing.

"I, um..."

Rob parked the SUV. "May I give you a call later and we can finalize? I don't have your number." Yeah, he could find it in the pageant marketing paperwork, but it was better to ask.

She pulled out an older model cell phone. "I'll record yours and text you. That work?"

"Sure." He recited the number. "So long as you don't forget to send me a text."

Bren's face flushed as she closed the app on her phone. "I won't forget. Promise."

"Okay then." He flashed her a smile and exited the vehicle to open her door. "Thanks for joining me this morning. I had a good time." He gave her a hand out and held it a second longer than required. Maybe some guys were first-date kissers, but not Rob. Definitely not with Bren, as skittish as she was. He walked her to the door and tipped his non-existent hat with a smile. "Have a great day."

The door shut behind her, and he strolled back to his SUV. As he slid in, his phone chimed with an incoming text.

Thanks for breakfast.

He grinned at the farmhouse in front of him. "The pleasure was all mine."

Chapter 6

"I was thinking I'd get the girls together on Saturday afternoons and teach them a deportment class." Marisa sat at the kitchen table. "What do you think?"

What Bren *thought* was that she wouldn't have to divulge her own plans this soon, before she knew what was going on with Rob. "What time? I might kind of have plans."

"Oh? Are the other farm families coming out tomorrow? I thought we'd set the field clean-up day for next week."

Bren traced the table's woodgrain with her finger. "No, not that. A... a friend invited me and the kids to Exploration World." Not that she'd said anything to Davy or Lila yet.

"Oh, cool! Who? Are you going with the Abercrombies?"

Bren shook her head. "Do you want a refill?"

"No, I'm floating in caffeine as it is." Marisa's eyes danced. "And now I'm dying of curiosity. Who are you going with?"

Bren topped off her coffee mug, not that she needed it. "Oh, just with Rob Santoro. He hasn't been." Had she sounded casual enough? She turned to set the pot back in the machine and took a second to stare out the window, hoping something — anything — would catch her eye so she could change the subject.

"Just Rob, huh? No big deal?"

Get a grip, Bren.

"Of course it's no big deal. He seems like a nice guy. He just wanted to do something nice for the kids."

"Not for you?"

"Me?" Bren turned, pressing her hand on her chest. "Of course not. What would a man like him see in a woman like me?" Although, he had texted her several times a day since Tuesday, asking how her day was going. Once he'd even sent her a link to a worship song he said he liked. *Good, Good Father* had lifted her spirits.

"I thought you were over that."

"Over what?"

"Over the guilt." Marisa's gaze caught Bren's and held.

Bren sighed. "It comes and goes, I'll be honest. Sometimes I look around and think how far I've come. I have you and your mom to thank for so much of that. And other times, I realize I'm still the person who botched her life so completely as a teenager there's no way to undo it."

"Life doesn't have a reset button."

Her heart sank a little. "Exactly."

"Did it ever occur to you that God might have allowed your experiences for a purpose?"

Bren lowered herself into her chair and lifted her coffee cup. "Why not prevent it, then? Instead of letting me make such a mess? Why couldn't I have remained pure and been able to look a man like Rob in the eye?"

"That's a lot of questions." Marisa sucked in her lip.

"Yeah, well, they're real. I know I'm saved. I'm grateful for it. But I'm still not the person I wish I could be."

"You know that Jesus doesn't look at you and say, *That Bren. If only I could save her from everything, but I'm not powerful enough. Some of her trash has to stay.*"

Bren grimaced and waved a hand. "Of course not."

"But that's what you're saying."

"No." Was she?

"That's what I hear."

"Marisa, how could you understand? You've lived a charmed life. Okay, your dad died, but at least he didn't beat your mother within an inch of her life and threaten you as well. You're gorgeous. You earned scholarships. You've modeled for big names in fashion. And, well, you're Miss Snowflake."

"All true."

"I'm not pretty. I flunked out of school. I messed up my life."

"The only one of those I'll grant you is flunking out of school."

"Oh, come on. Look at me."

Her friend reached across the table and covered Bren's hand with her own. "I'm looking at you, Bren Haddock."

Bren dared meet Marisa's gaze.

"I see someone who has made lemonade out of lemons. I see a pretty woman with fire and passion in her eyes. There's no need to be ashamed, Bren. Jesus has removed your sin as far as the east is from the west. Do you understand what that means?"

"I think so?"

"The psalmist didn't say as far as the north is from the south. Do you know why? If you keep going north, you'll eventually get to the North Pole, and every single direction is south from there. But if you keep going east, you'll never suddenly find yourself going west. It's not possible for those two directions to meet."

What did that even mean? Bren stared at Marisa while her brain massaged the words.

"That means God has put your sins so far away you can't trip over them again. The past happened, Bren, but it doesn't matter anymore. It really doesn't. You're a new person in Christ."

"I hear your words. I understand them." Bren touched her heart. "I don't know how to get them here."

"Prayer," said Marisa simply. "Dwelling in the Word and letting God speak His truth into your life."

"Don't you think I'm trying?"

"I know you are."

"Then... why? Why isn't there a magic button? Or maybe there is, but—"

"Bren."

She stared at Marisa. "What?"

"Life doesn't have a magic button only some people can find. Jesus' death on the cross is the only thing, and the results of that are open to everyone who believes. Then we keep learning more about Him and what He did for us so that we can grow as believers. We still mess up, and He continues to forgive us when we ask Him."

Bren took a deep breath. "I know that. I really do, but why is it so hard to remember?"

Marisa leaned closer, not letting Bren's eyes escape. "Because Satan knows you're a force to be reckoned with. He knows you have the experience and the ability to help other women."

Whoa. Could God really have a plan for her through this?

෴

"Hey, Rob, what time will you be home for Thanksgiving? Are you driving in Wednesday night?"

"Fran! I was going to give you a call soon." Like after his date with Bren and her kids tomorrow, if all went well. Rob valued his older sister's opinion and advice.

"What was holding you back?" She laughed. "Has the new job been keeping you that busy?"

He let warmth infuse his voice. "To answer your question, yes, I'll be in late Wednesday. I work until four and probably won't get out of Helena until after five."

"The kids are so excited to see you again."

"You mean Tieri." His little niece was five now. Even though he missed being part of her life, he couldn't see moving back to Spokane.

"Luca, too. Tieri is teaching him to say Uncle Rob. But it comes out more like Unkaroo."

Rob grinned. "Cute. I'll try to remember to answer to that."

"Will you stay with us? I'd love some time with you."

"Mom made it clear that I didn't have a choice. Guess I'm staying with them. Sorry."

"Hey, you're an adult. You can tell them."

"And see that wounded look on Mom's face? I can't make myself do it. But I promise I'll spend lots of time with you and Tad. I don't have to drive back until Sunday after lunch."

"So you'll come to church with us?"

"Wouldn't miss it." He'd been attending Helena Fellowship since he'd moved, but Bridgeview Bible would always be his home church. "Will you be playing piano for the service?"

"I don't think so. We've got a new guy, Logan Dermott, who's really talented and loves to play."

"Hey, don't let someone bump you out of your ministry spot."

"It's not like that." He could almost see Francesca waving her hand in dismissal. "I don't mind playing, but it was rough doing it every week. I never had enough time to practice. Now I can help out in other ways that suit me better."

"If you're sure."

"Oh, yeah, totally. I'm happy to worship without worrying about my fingers hitting all the right keys."

Rob shook his head, not that she could see. His sister astounded him with her easy-going nature, a quality he'd never quite managed to master.

"So what's new in your life? Have you met someone? Tieri keeps asking for cousins."

"Tell Tad's sisters that."

Fran chuckled. "She tells them herself."

The silence stretched while Rob debated whether his friendship with Bren was too new. It might not turn into anything.

"Rob? What are you not telling me?"

He never had been able to pull a fast one on his sister. "Okay, I'll admit it."

"Tell me everything!"

"It's kind of early, really." Rob thought of the many texts he and Bren had exchanged since breakfast a few days ago. "We've only gone out once."

"*Rob.*"

He took a deep breath. "Don't breathe a word to Mom and Dad. I mean it."

"Spit it out, little brother. Who is she?"

"Her name is Bren, and she's a single mom."

Fran squealed so loud Rob held his phone at arm's length while he rubbed his pained ear.

"How old are her kids? What does she do? Where did you meet?"

"Whoa, slow down. Davy is nine, and her d—"

"Oh, she's a cougar! Gotta watch out for those older women." Her voice was teasing.

"Not an older woman at all. She's twenty-six." He waited for Fran to do the math.

"Wow. Teen mom. That's rough."

"She's done a really good job parenting, especially since she met the Lord a few years ago."

"I'm glad she's a believer. You started to say something about a daughter?"

"Lila is seven. She's a good friend of my boss's daughter. That's how I met Bren."

"Tieri will be so excited."

"Please don't tell her. Not yet. I don't know how this is all going to work out, but I'm taking the three of them to the science museum tomorrow. I haven't spent any time at all with her son, and he might not want his mom seeing anyone. This is really weird. I never saw myself dating a woman with kids." The thought still unnerved him. It had been hard enough finding a woman who turned his head, but Bren's children created a much greater complexity.

"You'll win him over. You're great with kids, and what boy that age doesn't want a father?"

"Thanks. I'm taking it one step at a time, and we'll see how it goes." Oh, that sounded so controlled, so methodical, but it felt anything but. His entire world had tipped on its side, and he couldn't remember which side was up, or if he even cared.

"Hey, I have an idea."

Rob groaned.

"Why don't you bring them for Thanksgiving? You can stay with Mom and Dad if you must, and Bren and her kids can stay here."

"Uh, no. What part of *we've only been on one date* did you miss? This is way too soon to subject her to meeting the family." What would Bren's Thanksgiving be like, anyway? She wouldn't spend the day out at the farm alone with Davy and Lila, would she? No, he couldn't imagine Kristen's parents allowing that. They'd be well taken care of.

"Yeah, maybe." Fran's voice brightened. "How about Christmas? That gives you time for a whole bunch of dates."

He ran his finger around the suddenly constricting neck of his T-shirt. "Not sure I'll make it home for Christmas."

"You what? Rob, you can't miss. It's a family time... unless you're spending it with Bren?"

"I have to work Christmas Eve. We're doing a big marketing campaign for some beauty pageants, and I need to be at the final event to analyze results so I can build on the campaign for next year."

"Did I hear you say you're going to a beauty pageant on Christmas Eve? You're kidding me."

"You heard correctly. It's part of my job." He kept his voice steady.

"Is Bren in it?" Fran asked coyly.

Here went nothing. "No. Her daughter is."

"No way. Get out of their lives. Seriously. You don't want to date a Crowns for Kids kind of mother. They're obsessed with all the wrong things. They—"

"*Francesca.*"

She stopped.

"It's not like that. Trust me to have a little sense, would you?"

Fran let a long breath out into the phone. "I'll try, but be really careful. I have a bad feeling about this. I didn't know you were getting desperate."

"I'm not. I really like Bren a lot, and she's very down-to-earth. She's so down-to-earth she manages a farm for a CSA box program."

"Pictures, Rob. I need to see her. I'll be able to tell."

"Trust me, sis."

"I'll try, but it's hard. You're twenty-eight and never been in a serious relationship, at least not one you told me about. There's a lot riding on this."

A laugh escaped. "You think I don't know that? I'm open to your prayers, but no meddling, and definitely no telling anyone else until there's something more to tell. Promise?"

"Mom could talk some sense into you."

"Francesca."

"Fine. But if you're still dating her when you're home at Thanksgiving, you'd better let our parents know, or I will. Two weeks is long enough for your little secret."

"It's a deal."

Chapter 7

*Y*ou two had better behave yourselves." Bren squeezed Lila's and Davy's shoulders as Rob's SUV turned into the driveway. "Remember to say thank you for taking us to the museum."

Davy shrugged out of her grasp. "I'm always good."

Lila beamed up at Bren. "I'm a little angel, right, Mommy?"

Yeah, right, on both counts. "Get your parkas on. We don't want him to have to wait for us."

Davy paused with one arm down his sleeve. "What do you think I'm doing?"

"No back talk." Even as she said it, Bren cringed. "Sorry, bucko. I'm just nervous."

Her little boy pulled his eyebrows together. "Why? It's a museum."

"Because it's *Rob*, silly." Lila rolled her eyes. "Mom wants him to like us."

Davy shook his head.

Bren could about hear his thoughts. *What's the big deal? What's not to like?* If only she still had the innocence of her children. Marisa's words from the day before filtered into her mind as she put on her own jacket. Saved by Jesus. She could do this.

The doorbell rang, and Baxter gave one half-hearted woof from his mat in the kitchen. Lila ran back to give the old dog a hug. "We'll be back soon."

Bren opened the door. The sight of Rob Santoro on her doorstep took her breath away. How had a man so handsome, so kind, come into her life? She didn't deserve — *saved by Jesus*.

His eyes crinkled as he looked deeply into hers, as he smiled at her. "Good morning, Bren."

"Hi, Rob." She nudged Davy forward. "This is my son, Davy. Davy, this is Rob."

"Pleased to meet you, Davy." Rob stuck out his hand as her son, hands in his pockets, gave Rob a once-over.

After a long, humiliating moment, Davy nodded and shook Rob's hand. "Same to you."

Lila slid back into the entryway on sock feet. "Hi, Rob! Are we really going to Exploration World? I can't wait. Me an' Davy have wanted to go forever, but Mom kept saying no."

Rob slid a glance Bren's way, but she reached for the zip on Lila's jacket. "Here you go, sweetie. Let's get going."

"We really are, Lila." Rob opened the door behind him and the kids poured past him.

Davy stopped on the top step. "Nice wheels. Four-wheel drive?"

"Yes, I like getting out into the mountains." Rob might be answering her son, but he grinned at Bren, his face still fully smiling. "Back country backpacking and stuff."

The kids hadn't scared him off yet? That whole man-to-man thing Davy was trying to put on? Maybe she could breathe after all.

Davy turned and looked up at Rob. "Like sleeping in a tent?"

That was more the little boy she knew, eager for adventures.

"Yes, like that. There are some great trails in Glacier National Park. Places you can hike along a mountain stream and climb so high it feels like you might be in heaven."

This man made roughing it sound like fun. This man could make anything sound like fun.

"Hop in." Rob opened one backdoor and gestured to Lila.

"There are angels in heaven," she informed him. "I'm an angel on earth."

He tweaked her nose. "I saw your costume at Halloween, remember? You were a cute little angel." He closed the door and opened the front one, which he'd been partially blocking.

Once again her gaze caught Rob's. He was so good with her kids, at least now, before Lila's whining and

73

Davy's attitude got to him. No, she wouldn't think the worst. She gave him a tentative smile and accepted his help as she climbed into the front seat. The warmth from his fingers lingered as he rounded the vehicle and slid into the driver's side.

He caught her staring and gave her a slow wink. Her face flushed. Hopefully neither of the kids had caught that one.

***

"What was the best part, Davy?" asked Bren.

They were seated at lunch, and Rob had managed to slide into the booth next to Bren, leaving two excited children on the opposite bench. The waitress set burgers in front of each of them.

The boy's eyes lit up. "Everything! Except the Farm to Fork area, because I already know all about that from home."

"I liked that part," announced Lila. "I liked to pretend cook. Can I help real cook, Mommy?"

"I'm sure I can use your help."

"The outdoors exhibit," went on Davy. "Someday I want to go camping for real." He eyed Rob.

How was he supposed to answer that? "I'm sure someday you will."

"Will you take me?"

Kids. They certainly added a new dimension. Testing it before it had a chance to gel on its own. What was the best answer? Rob could feel Bren shifting slightly on the bench beside him. She was probably afraid of his answer. No more than he was, for sure.

On the other hand, a boy Davy's age needed a man in his life, even if that man wasn't married to his mother. Even if things didn't keep moving forward with Bren, that didn't mean he couldn't take the boy camping once or twice, right?

"I don't see any reason why we couldn't do that," Rob said cautiously. "But it's a long time until summer."

"Me, too." Lila's eyes pleaded from across the table. "I want to go camping, too."

Davy's chest puffed out as he turned to his little sister. "It's a guy thing."

The sensation of drowning nearly overwhelmed Rob. "Girls can go camping, too." He didn't dare look at Bren. Did she even like that sort of thing? Maybe not, if she'd never taken her children. But it might have been lack of money talking. That was the only reason he could think of why Davy and Lila hadn't ever been to Exploration World. It wasn't expensive, but might've been above her budget.

Had it been a good idea to invite the kids along on their second date? If he were going to keep moving forward with Bren, the children had to be on board. But maybe he was moving too quickly. He thought of his sister's phone call. Although he was too slow for some people.

"This is good. Thanks, Rob." Davy set the burger back on his plate and picked up his drink.

"Yes, thank you," piped up Lila, peeking at her mother.

"You're welcome." Man, if this felt like a lot of pressure to Rob, what must it feel like to Bren? He barely dared glance at her for fear he'd lose himself in her eyes in front of the children. That would bring more questions he couldn't answer. No more dates with the two of them along for a while.

Rob shifted over a couple of inches until his thigh touched Bren's. She didn't move away. This might have to do for right now. After today, he was pretty sure he could win her kids all the way over. But what about Bren? Would she remain cautious, or was she winnable?

Bren pushed open the door to the formal reception room at Grizzly Gulch Resort. "Have a good time, sweetie." She bent to press a kiss on Lila's forehead.

"Hey, Bren!" Marisa, seated cross-legged on the stage floor, waved. "Are you going to stay?"

"Not today, if that's okay."

"Um, sure. No problem. You've got Davy?"

Her son and more. "Yep. What time shall I pick up Lila?"

Marisa checked her watch. "Two hours?"

"Sounds good."

Lila, Charlotte, and two other little girls were already dancing in a circle. There was no need for Bren to stay. Marisa hadn't asked her to, had she? No. It was fine. But it would be more inside her comfort zone to work with the children than to return to the SUV where her son grilled Rob about fishing.

She made her way back through the inn's spacious foyer and out to the portico. Rob met her beside the vehicle and opened the door for her. He was so thoughtful.

"How come you did that?" asked Davy as Rob entered the other side. "My mom knows how to open a door."

Rob turned in his seat to face the boy. "I know she can, but it's a little something men can do to show they are gentlemen."

Bren didn't need to see Davy's face to visualize the confusion. "What do you mean?"

"Gentlemen have good manners. They open doors, and they let the lady go first. Gentlemen also offer to carry things for ladies and help them with their jackets or with chairs."

"I know I'm not supposed to punch girls."

Bren bit the insides of her cheeks to keep from laughing. Davy could obviously use someone around to teach him how to be a man. In her periphery, she saw Rob grin in her direction before looking back at Davy.

"Good start, buddy. That's part of being a gentleman, too."

Davy sighed. "It sounds like a lot of things to remember."

Rob chuckled. "Sometimes it is. Like with anything else, though, practice makes perfect." He turned to Bren and lowered his voice. "I hate to think of taking you home yet."

Her, too. It had been an idyllic day, and she didn't want it to end. She gave him a small smile. "There's no reason you can't come in for a while. I don't have to come back for Lila for two hours." She'd think of some way to snatch a few child-free moments in that amount of time.

"I'd like that," Rob said softly as he put the SUV in gear.

A few minutes later they were back at the farm. As Bren had suspected, it only took one mention of video games to send Davy dashing into the living room. Which meant she couldn't sit on the sofa with Rob.

"Come on in the kitchen," she offered. "I'll put on a coffee." This was better anyway. She could find something to do that didn't require sitting and staring at this gorgeous guy. Even though she wanted to do just that.

Rob followed her through the dining room. "This is a nice place. Homey."

"It is. We're very lucky to live here. It sure beats the two-bedroom apartment we were in until the beginning of this year." She bit her lip. It was like she had to keep reminding him.

"I bet. You mentioned Marisa's mom owns it? Is she thinking of selling?"

Bren measured coffee grounds and dumped them in the filter. "Not anytime soon that I know of. I'm contracted to manage the farm for at least one more growing season."

Rob took a stool at the kitchen island. "It reminds me a bit of my nonna's house in Spokane. Big kitchen."

She poured water into the reservoir, flipped the switch, then leaned back on the counter, facing him. "When we're in the middle of canning tomatoes, there still doesn't seem to be enough counter space."

His face crinkled with his ready smile. "I bet. Nonna cans a lot, too, including about five kinds of pasta sauce. I guess it's the Italian thing to do."

"My kids and I subsisted on mac and cheese for too long. I can't imagine what I was thinking with all the junk I fed them."

"You were thinking full bellies were better than hungry bellies." His gaze didn't falter.

"Yeah. Something like that. Now, with a big garden and actually learning how to cook, things are so much better."

"I know what you mean."

Bren's eyebrows rose. "You can cook?"

"Sure, why not? I'm twenty-eight. My mom made sure I knew the basics before I left for college. I can't tell you all the heartache — to say nothing of gut-ache — she spared me."

"Name one thing you can cook."

"One thing?" He burst out laughing. "Come on, girl. I have a bigger repertoire than that."

She lifted her chin.

"Okay, I make a mean pasta sauce, thanks to Nonna. Want me to prove it?" Rob's eyes challenged hers.

Uh oh. Had she just been finagling more time with him? Well, so what if she had? "Yes, I do. What specialty ingredients do you need?" Probably something she didn't have.

"Tomatoes. Onions. Garlic. Basil and oregano, fresh if possible. Italian sausages."

"We were good up through the herbs, but I don't have Italian sausages."

"Let me have a look at your spice shelf, and I'll run into Super One Foods for meat and anything else we need. Unless you had other plans for supper."

Bren tipped her head and looked over at him. He wasn't going to run from her challenge?

Rob grinned. "Deal?" He held up his right hand above the island as he leaned toward her.

She slapped his hand in a high-five. "Deal."

His fingers caught around hers, caressing them. His eyes — oh, goodness, those eyes — nearly melted her on the spot.

The sputtering coffee pot and the squealing of incoming missiles from the living room broke the moment.

Was she crazy to think that this gorgeous man might be all he seemed to be... and that he might stay interested in her despite the mess in her life? Because if she wasn't deluded, her future might be a lot rosier than she'd begun to think possible, to say nothing of tastier.

Chapter 8

Rob couldn't help the whistle when Bren flipped on the light in her back porch. Nonna would definitely approve of this woman once she saw all this canning. "Wow, you have been busy."

Beside him, Bren rubbed her hands together, more nervousness than glee by the expression on her face. "Yeah. It was a lot of work, but we will eat like royalty."

Gleaming glass jars filled one wall from floor to ceiling. Pickles, fruit, and soup — she must have a pressure canner tucked in a cupboard somewhere — marched in colorful rows, but the crowning glory, in his opinion, was the abundance of canned tomatoes. Chunked tomatoes, whole plum tomatoes in juice, pureed tomatoes... a slice of Italian heaven.

For a moment he'd felt guilt at using any of her ingredients, but not anymore. She had plenty to spare. "Let's take three quarts of the plum tomatoes, several onions, and a bulb of garlic."

She plucked garlic the size of her fist from a basket.

"Okay, half of one of those. Wow. Your soil must love garlic." He gathered the jars and set them on the kitchen counter, and she followed a moment later with the alliums.

"You're really going to cook dinner for us?"

Bren stood so near he could smell her faint perfume and feel the heat from her arm. He raised his brows and looked deeply into her brown eyes. "Are you retracting the invitation?" he asked softly.

Her eyes flared slightly. She seemed as aware of him as he was of her.

Rob turned and set both hands on her shoulders. "Because I'm a very good cook," he murmured. "I want to make you a meal you won't ever forget."

"I won't forget. No man has ever done this for me before."

"I'm hoping this dinner will be the first of many."

She bit her lip. "I'd like that."

Rob's hands slid down her back and onto her hips. "I would, too." He fought the desire to gather her all the way into his arms and kiss her. That moment was coming, but it wasn't now with Davy in the next room shouting at the game console as he took down another missile. He rubbed her back for a few seconds then stepped back.

Surely his face revealed the same wonder and disappointment reflected on Bren's. He offered a lopsided smile and turned to the task at hand. "Let's see what you've got for a big heavy-bottomed pot."

She opened the base cabinet beside the stove and gestured at him to have a look. Her cookware looked thin and not the best quality. Maybe he'd get her a cast-iron Dutch oven, lined with porcelain, for Christmas.

Maybe he'd get her a diamond ring.

Rob nearly dropped the large pot in his hands. A ring? Was he really falling so fast and so hard that he was thinking of marriage after only knowing Bren for a few weeks? That was crazy talk. Yet his dad had always told him that when he met the right woman, he'd have no doubt. Dad should know. His marriage to Mom had taken place when they'd known each other only three weeks... thirty-seven years back. Rob had always thought they were just lucky. Now he wasn't so sure. He could see himself and Bren with graying hair, still looking at each other like—

Was he staring at her? Was she creeped out by the intensity in his gaze? He blinked her face into focus.

"You okay, Rob? It seemed like you zoned out for a minute."

He set the pot on the stove top and reached for her hands. "I kind of did. I'm okay, though." He caressed her fingers. "I've never been better."

Her lips parted as though they realized they were the center of his attention.

"Bam!" yelled Davy.

Bren's gaze flicked to the living room then to Rob. She stepped back until she bumped into the island.

Rob grinned at her ruefully. He wanted to kiss her. Taste her. Savor her. More than once. Later. More mundane things called now, though. "Olive oil?"

His words broke the spell.

"Um, yes." Bren opened a tall pantry cupboard beside the fridge. "In here. Herbs, too." She glanced at him, her cheeks flushed and eyes bright. "I'll be right back." Her feet pounded up the stairs and a door above opened and closed.

Rob took a deep breath. Maybe now he could think for a few minutes. It would never do to mess up this dinner when he was trying so hard to impress her. To impress her kids. That meant not only remembering the recipe in his head, but keeping the sauce from burning in this thin-bottomed pot. Low heat. Patience. Lots of stirring.

Maybe not unlike wooing the woman he was falling for.

He could do this. On both counts.

⌒◡◠

Bren leaned against the back wall of the resort's reception room and watched eight youngsters cross the stage in single file, pausing in the center to curtsy to an invisible audience. Lila was as flawless as any of them. Bren blinked back tears. Her little girl was growing up. Whether the pageant was hurrying that along or simply coming alongside didn't seem relevant at the moment. Just like Davy needed a man like Rob to teach him how to be a gentleman, so Lila needed to be taught manners and poise. Why not have a little fun with her peers while she was at it?

The girls gathered into a circle around Marisa.

Bren couldn't hear what her friend was saying from over here, but Marisa's face was intent as she spoke, looking at each little girl in turn. They nodded their heads, feet constantly in motion. Then they broke ranks and ran toward the waiting parents.

Marisa's gaze caught Bren's from across the room. She waved her over.

Well, why not? Keeping some distance from Rob Santoro for a bit longer was a good idea. That man turned her inside out like no one ever had. Imagine a gorgeous man in her kitchen, giving her smoldering looks while teaching her son how to chop an onion. He'd even taken Davy on a quick run to the supermarket, and hadn't let Bren look in the bags when they returned. What mystery ingredients had he picked up? No, it was best to stay away for a few minutes longer.

"Lila did really well this afternoon." Marisa rested a hand on the girl's shoulder. "She's got natural grace."

Bren blinked. "Really? That's great." She tugged Lila to her side. "Did you have fun, sweetie?"

Lila nodded, her eyes dancing. "Should I get my coat on, Mommy?"

"Yes, please do."

Marisa eyed Bren as Lila scampered away. "So what did you do with your free afternoon?"

"I, uh, I..."

Her friend's eyebrows rose. "Lila talked a lot about Rob and the museum."

"Um."

Marisa leaned closer. "You spent all day with him?"

85

Heat rolled up Bren's cheeks. "Yes? Is that bad?"

"Whoa. He is one fast moving dude."

She'd thought the same thing once or twice herself. "Today has been all about him getting to know the kids." Maybe she could convince herself if she tried hard enough. "He and Davy are cooking supper in my kitchen right now."

"The man can cook? Don't let him get away."

"He says he can. Guess we'll see."

Marisa smiled. "I'm so happy for you, Bren. You deserve a great guy like Rob."

"I don't *deserve*—"

Her friend held up a finger. "Don't say it. Remember who Jesus says you are."

"I am telling myself that a hundred times a day."

"Good. I wish Jase could cook. As a fashion photographer, he's usually on location then eating out when at home base." Marisa grimaced. "I've been not much better this past year."

"But you taught me—"

"I know. But I haven't been doing that much of it myself. Life has been incredibly busy what with all the Miss Snowflake events this year. But enough about me. Tell me more about Rob."

Bren glanced around to see Lila and Charlotte chattering like magpies halfway across the large room. "I don't know what to say. He's pretty amazing."

Marisa lowered her voice. "Has he kissed you?"

The simmering heat exploded on Bren's cheeks. "No." But by the intensity in Rob's gaze a time or two, he'd been thinking about it.

"Are you going to let him?"

"Maybe." Oh, yeah. And she'd give it right back. "If the kids aren't around."

Marisa giggled. "I bet he's smarter than that. Bren, promise me you'll give him a real chance. Don't duck away because you think he's some saint. He may be amazing, but he'll prove to you soon enough that he's not perfect."

Rob? Not perfect? Oh, Bren knew he wasn't, but only because no humans were. She couldn't imagine an angry or mean word coming from his mouth. Couldn't imagine him acting selfishly. "It sounds like you think you're hearing my wedding bells. We're going to take this nice and slow. In a year or two, we'll see how it's going."

Where were those words even coming from? Who waited that long if they knew they'd met the right person? Bren certainly never had in the past. For a few years she'd hopped into bed with any guy who'd wanted to be there. All the more reason to hold back with Rob. Not just on the sex side, but in the whole relationship thing.

"A year or two? You have got to be kidding me. Let me tell you how hard a year-long engagement has been on me and Jase."

Bren held up her hand. "I don't want to know."

"Well, it's been brutal. We've been so tempted I can't even describe it. So many times I was ready to toss my tiara back at the pageant board and let my runner-up have it for the rest of the year so I could elope with Jase. And, yes, there were times I desperately wanted to give myself to him and hope no one found out. But God would know."

Bren made a show of sticking her fingers in her ears. "La la la."

Marisa leaned in. "So don't even talk to me about waiting a year or two like it's no big deal. You guys aren't eighteen. When you know, you know, and then you get married. Why push yourself to withstand temptation if you don't have to?"

"I. Uh."

"You might not be an angel, but none of us are. Still, you and I are both God's cherished princesses. Because Jesus paid for our sins, we deserve what He deserves. Life and love."

Oh, to have Marisa's confidence. "Thanks," Bren whispered.

"You got it, girl. Now you take Lila and go home, and don't let that man get away tonight without a kiss, you hear? Even if you have to get it started yourself. Life's too short."

Bren thought on Marisa's words the whole way home. She and Lila entered a house smelling of spicy meat, tomatoes, and delectable herbs. Her friend was right. She'd be crazy to let this guy get away.

Maybe she should send the kids upstairs or outside for a bit. But as soon as she entered the kitchen, that thought faded away.

Davy stood beside the island, biting his lip as he rolled a long thin piece of dough on the counter with his palms.

Rob stood behind him, hands over Davy's, helping. "Just like that."

Bren might have been frozen in the doorway, but Lila wasn't. She bounced into the room and up onto one of the tall stools across the island. "Whatcha doing? Can I help?"

"We're making dessert." Davy didn't look up. "It's a guy thing."

Rob met Bren's gaze. His eyes warmed and those little crinkles she was growing to love spread across his face.

Did he know what he was doing to her, arms braced around her son, teaching him?

"What kind of dessert? Can I taste?"

Davy shot Lila an irritated look. "It doesn't taste like anything yet. Just dough. It's called..." He glanced up at Rob. "I can't remember how to pronounce it."

"Struffoli." Rob grinned down at the boy. "They're kind of like doughnut holes drenched in honey."

Lila jiggled on the tall stool. "Yum! I love doughnuts."

"Did you have a good time with Marisa?" Rob asked, looking at Lila.

"Yes! I can walk like a lady now. And curtsy."

Rob grinned. "Can I see?"

Bren couldn't tear her gaze away from Rob's face as he watched her daughter. Her heart was full. So full. Could Rob really step into her family this easily? Provide the father figure her kids needed so badly? Could he complete not only her family... but her?

He turned back to Davy. "Those are great. They have to rest now, and we'll cut them up and fry them this evening. Okay?"

Davy nodded. "Can I do that part, too?"

Bren held her breath.

"No, sorry, buddy. I'd better do the hot oil part. You can watch, though. But that's for later."

Davy scrubbed his hands under the kitchen faucet. "Hey, Lila. I beat another level of Asteroid Attacker. Want to see?"

"Yeah!"

The two kids ricocheted out of the kitchen, leaving Bren staring at Rob, aware of the simmering pasta sauce. The simmering eyes looking right back at her.

She rounded the island and stretched both hands toward him. "Thank you."

Rob pulled her close. "For what?"

"For... I don't know. For spending time with Davy. For making Lila feel like a princess."

He tucked one finger under her chin, encouraging her to look up even as her arms went around his middle. "And for you?"

"Making me feel like I'm worth something, even with a tarnished halo."

"Bren." His voice was low, his gaze intent. "You are worth a lot. More than I could ever say. May I kiss you?"

She nodded, her lips already trembling, as she tipped her face toward his.

Rob's mouth covered hers, and she melted against his solid chest. For the first time in her life, the sensation of being kissed came with the feelings of complete respect, of being cherished. Of being enough.

Chapter 9

*T*odd leaned back in his chair and leveled a look at Rob. "You want to come in late for work once a week? What's up with that?"

Was there any hint of understanding in his boss's gaze? "I made up the time last week. Stayed late and got in both my hours and the proposal for The Parrot Confectionary."

"What's so important on Tuesday mornings?"

"Seeing Bren when her children are in school and we can get some time to ourselves." Rob held up a hand. "At breakfast in a public place."

There did seem to be a faint twinkle in Todd's eyes. "So you're going along with Kristen's matchmaking?"

"I'm thankful for the introduction, but I'm not *going along with* anything. I happen to like Bren." He paused. "Quite a lot."

"The thought of taking on some other man's kids isn't an issue?"

Rob kept his voice even. "Not at all. I'll admit I wondered about that a few weeks ago, but not anymore. Bren hasn't had contact with their dads in years. Both men signed away parental rights."

Todd's eyebrows rose. "I didn't realize they didn't share a father."

"No. Bren didn't know the Lord." Rob wasn't surprised it was an issue for Todd. It would have bothered him, too, if asked the question theoretically a month or more ago. "She became a Christian about three years ago now, and she's a new person in Jesus."

"I like Bren. Don't get me wrong. I just want to make sure you know where you're going with this. I don't want to see her hurt."

Rob kept his gaze steady. "I have no intention of hurting her. You're right that she's somewhat vulnerable. I know I need to tread carefully, but I also know there's nothing to gain if I worry too much about it." He glanced over his shoulder and nudged the office door shut. "The honest truth?"

"Yes?"

"I get that it's a bit early to know, but I honestly believe God brought us together. I'd never dreamed of marrying a woman like Bren. As of this past week, I can't imagine marrying anyone else."

Todd let out a low whistle. "You're in deep."

"I'm twenty-eight. My heart has been waiting for her. God brought me to Helena when we were both ready."

"So a weekly breakfast date?"

"With your permission."

Todd cracked a smile. "I'd hate to block the path of true love. I do need the stats for the Downtown Association's Christmas promotion on my desk Wednesday morning, though. And the Miss Snowflake Pageant contestant booklet by end-of-day Friday."

"Done and done. I've looked at next week's deadlines, too. There shouldn't be any problem getting things wrapped up before I leave for Spokane."

"You taking Bren to meet your parents over Thanksgiving?"

Rob shook his head. "She mentioned something about visiting a friend in Kennewick for the weekend, so I didn't push her. I'm not sure if she's ready for my relatives yet."

"Or you're not ready?"

"Todd, I don't know how big your family is, but mine's pretty intense. My grandmother, my parents, my sister and her husband and kids, my dad's four brothers, and all *their* families live within a few blocks of each other. One big, noisy, Italian family."

Todd grinned. "And you couldn't wait to get away from them."

"Yeah, there's that. I'm an introvert in a sea of extroverts." He held up a hand. "And, yes, I know Bren is far more outgoing than I am. Still, that's a lot of strangers, all avidly focused on her. Just seems like we should be a little more — I don't know... secure? — before tackling the big meet-the-family event."

"They can't be that bad."

Rob shook his head. "You haven't met my nonna. She runs that whole neighborhood, Santoros and others alike."

93

"I can't believe you're afraid of an old lady."

Rob chuckled. "Not afraid, exactly. It's just she made up her mind years ago whom I should marry, and she hasn't let up. I ignore her, which is fine, but it doesn't stop her pushing. Bren doesn't need Nonna's opinions flung in her face at this stage."

"Don't wait too long, man. Sounds like your grandmother will need time to adjust. Maybe you should have a heart-to-heart over the long weekend."

"I'm sure it will come up."

"Okay. Tuesdays you'll be in at ten instead of eight, until further notice?"

"Please and thanks." Rob stretched his hand out and gave Todd's a firm shake. "I'll make up those two hours for sure."

                        ∽‍‍‍

"Sounds like it's a good thing we met late in the fall," Rob said over breakfast the next day.

Bren laughed. "You've got it. From April through October it's crazy busy on the farm. I'm going from morning to night every day except Sunday but, even then, it's hard to take a full day off."

"I signed up for a CSA basket when I lived in Billings. I never stopped to wonder what all the farmers' daily lives looked like."

"If they do it as a full time business like we do at Hiller Farm, there's no end to weeding, watering, and picking. Marisa used to have to deliver everything to a drop-off point but this summer Bob Delaney started going around the farms twice a week and picking up the produce. That saves a lot of time. He's got a whole team of volunteers to sort, pack, and deliver the boxes on Tuesdays and Fridays."

"Sounds crazy intense."

Bren poked at her fruit cup. "It is. It's pretty rewarding, though. I don't take food as much for granted as I used to."

"I imagine not. So what will you do with all your free time over the winter?"

In the past two weeks, she'd spent a lot of it with Rob. Hopefully that would continue. "I'll finish two college courses and have some girl time. I haven't seen a lot of my friends since spring, unless they've come to the farm and pitched in."

His hand touched hers across the table. "Your energy amazes me."

"There's so much to do." If he only knew. "Davy and Lila have kids' club at church on Tuesday evenings, and I've got ladies' Bible study on Thursday mornings. Then I need to run Davy to skating and Lila to gymnastics, plus a visit to the library nearly every week. Sometimes it's a nuisance living out of town." She thought back to previous years. "But we have a bigger place to live, so it's all good." She gave him a bright smile. "How about you?"

Rob shook his head. "I'm a complete slouch compared to you. Most days I go home from work, go for a run or bike ride, fix a bite to eat, then read or watch TV. Boring stuff."

She angled her head at him. "Sounds... quiet."

He grinned. "Compared to your life? Definitely."

"But you kind of like quiet."

"So easy to tell?" His eyebrows peaked.

Bren grinned. "Yes? You've been in Helena since August? How many friends have you made? I mean, besides Todd."

"Todd's my boss."

"Well, of course. But he can still be a friend. Anyone else?"

Rob scratched the back of his neck. "Uh... Jase?"

"Oh, I didn't know you guys were hanging out! Cool."

"Not hanging out, exactly."

Bren narrowed her gaze at him. "Friends do stuff together."

"I do stuff with you." His hand covered hers on the table. "Plus I work full time."

"But before you met me. You've been in Helena for months."

"Didn't we cover that? Bike rides. Hikes."

"With whom?"

"By myself."

He didn't seem to get it. "But you need friends. Have you been going to the men's prayer breakfast at church? That's Fridays, right?"

"Bren, I'm not like you. I know you thrive on having a lot of people around you, but I don't. I like being with you. I like your kids. I even like your friends, but that doesn't mean I can change who I am at the core. I'll always need time to recharge."

"But even the Bible says we shouldn't forsake gathering together."

The skin around Rob's eyes crinkled as he grinned at her. "That verse in Hebrews is talking about corporate worship. I rarely miss a Sunday morning. It's not that I don't appreciate meeting God surrounded by His people. I do. I'm uplifted by the singing and challenged by the preaching. I'm humbled when little old ladies come over and tell me they're praying for me."

Bren giggled. "Mrs. Abercrombie?"

"Yes, I think so."

"What did you say?"

"I thanked her, of course. A guy can't have too many people praying for him."

"I love her, but she's a bit of a busybody."

Rob shrugged. "I don't mind. Just because I'm not super outgoing doesn't mean I want to be invisible."

"No one wants to be invisible." She'd always thought quiet people were just too shy to jump into the center of attention, but secretly wished to be there. Huh. Maybe not. Maybe she'd been guilty of pushing more than one friend to be someone they weren't. Or trying to, anyway. It hadn't always gone well.

His warm fingers caressed hers, and his thumb fiddled with hers.

Why would she want to change him? Wasn't he awesome the way he was? Gentle. Kind. So handsome he put her gut in a knot when he looked at her the way he did now, like she was the center of the universe. Wasn't it better to be that for one person in private than for many at a party?

"What are you thinking?" Rob asked softly.

"You're perfect," she blurted.

He smiled, but his head was shaking. "So far from it, Bren. I'm just like everyone else in the church, a sinner saved by the grace of God, and so thankful for it. Striving to be more like Jesus, but failing every day."

"Name one thing."

"What?" He pulled back, looking at her with a puzzled expression.

"One way you're not perfect, because I don't see it."

"Bren." His deep eyes would not release hers. "Don't put me on a pedestal. I'll disappoint you. I promise. If not today, then next week."

He was right. Maybe it was just love blinding her. Love? Had she known him long enough to have those sorts of feelings for him? But love was fickle.

"I'm stubborn, Bren. Willful. I have a big problem with pride."

"But that's nothing compared to my sins. I mean, unless you've been stoned and slept around and got a few girls pregnant and just didn't tell me yet."

His gaze remained steady. "No, I haven't done those things. Well, I drank too much a few times and decided it wasn't worth the headache."

"See?"

"That doesn't make me perfect, Bren. There are plenty of ways to sin. Remember that verse in Romans? *For everyone has sinned; we all fall short of God's glorious standard.*"

"Yeah, but..."

"There is no but. You know Jesus is the only one who's perfect. The rest of us are far from measuring up." He looked at her thoughtfully. "Let's say we had to get to Hawaii by swimming." He laughed. "I'll make it easy for you, and let you start in Oregon instead of Montana. How far would you get?"

"Uh... not far."

"Me, neither. I'd still be in sight of land when I drowned. How about an Olympic distance swimmer?"

"Well, Michael Phelps would get a whole lot further than me."

"All the way to Hawaii?"

Bren swatted the back of his hand lightly. "Of course not. It's impossible."

"So if that's the standard, and neither you and Phelps reach it, does it matter if he made it a mile or two further than you did? You're both in the same boat. Or lack of one."

She chuckled. "Okay, I get what you're saying. It's just..."

"Bren?" His brown eyes deepened until she could drown in them. "It's not Jesus telling you you're not good enough. It's never been about being good enough. Jesus covers it. Period."

In her mind's eye, Bren touched the tarnished, broken halo on her head. Could she let go of the imagery, once for all, and remember who she was in Christ?

Chapter 10

"How come Rob's coming over again, Mommy?" Lila set silverware on the table. "Doesn't he have a kitchen at his house?"

"I'm sure he does." Not that Bren had seen Rob's apartment. She assumed it would be like any other bachelor suite she'd seen, but that was probably doing him a disservice, from how well he cooked. Not only that, but a messy man wouldn't load the dishwasher and scrub pots at his girlfriend's house as a matter of course, would he?

His girlfriend. She was Rob Santoro's girlfriend. Every evening she went to bed marveling that she hadn't scared him off yet.

"Then why, Mom?" insisted Lila.

How to explain grownup romance to a seven-year-old? Bren couldn't bring herself to try. She tweaked Lila's pigtail. "Because he likes us, I guess. Maybe he gets lonely all by himself at his apartment."

A cold wind accompanied Davy and Baxter in the back door. "What smells good?"

Always a hearty eater, the kid was difficult to fill up lately. He was sure growing.

"I have meatloaf in the oven, along with baked potatoes and a red kuri squash."

"Mmm. Do I have time to play Asteroid Attacker before supper?" He rubbed his tummy as though undecided which he preferred.

Bren glanced at the clock. "Maybe a few minutes. Everything is pretty much done, and Rob will be here soon." Besides taking her out for breakfast on Tuesdays, he'd been by for supper several times — sometimes early enough to help cook — and stayed long after reading bedtime stories to the kids.

She was afraid to think long-term, but the habits were looking good for now.

"I see his car!" called Lila from the living room window.

"It's not a car." Davy sighed. "It's an SUV. That means sports utility vehicle."

"I just call it a car."

Bren grinned, her stomach fluttering as it always did at his arrival. He never had to knock, as one of the kids always flung the door open for him. This time it was Lila.

"Hi, Rob. Why are you here again? Don't you have food at your house?"

"Sure do, munchkin. I'm here to see you and your mom." The door clicked shut.

"Why do you want to see my mom?"

Around the corner in the kitchen, Bren held her breath and strained her ears.

Rob lowered his voice. "Can I tell you a secret?"

"Yes!"

"I like your mom a lot."

Bren bit her lip and pressed her hands to the counter top.

"Is that why you bring her pretty flowers?"

Had he really brought a fresh bouquet? He didn't need to do that. The last one was still gorgeous, and she was heading out of town tomorrow.

"I bring them because she's a very special lady. You know that?"

"Yeah, she's my mom. I don't have a dad."

"Every girl needs a dad, I think."

Oh, my goodness. No way was she ready to go there. Supper. She needed to get it on the table. Bren whirled, grabbed a pair of heat-resistant pads, and opened the oven.

"Here, can I help?" Rob's voice was so near she almost dropped the pan of meatloaf.

"Sure. Thanks." She didn't dare meet his gaze as he took the oven mitts from her. Was it hot in here, or was it just her? Tendrils of hair clung to her forehead and neck.

Rob chuckled as he set the pan of squash on the stove top. "You must have been eavesdropping."

"Um..." No use in denying it. "I heard."

"It's only true."

Bren looked past him to see two pairs of eyes watching with curiosity. Beyond them, the vibrant arrangement of dahlias and daisies from a few days ago graced the center of the table. Was it wrong to be disappointed? "I thought you'd brought more." Oh, man, that sounded so greedy of her.

"More what?" He expertly transferred the chunks of squash to a serving bowl.

She should be helping. "Flowers. You're spoiling me, but I'm glad you remembered we were going to be away and didn't need a fresh bouquet."

Rob quirked a lopsided grin in her direction. "I'll bring more on Monday, when we're back. It's fun spoiling you. When was the last time anyone did?"

Her face flushed.

"Exactly." He turned toward her, his back to the children. "I like being your one and only," he whispered then puckered his lips in a pretend kiss.

Bren felt her eyes widen. It was all she could do not to take three steps forward, wrap her arms around him, and kiss him for real.

Rob winked. "Who wants to carry this bowl to the table?"

"Me!" shouted both children.

"Here, Lila. Davy, I'll get you the next one in just a sec." He reached back into the oven and rescued the rest of supper before glancing back at Bren. "Do you need anything else?"

Just you.

Bren pulled her thoughts together. "Thanks. Let's eat while it's hot."

At the table, they all reached for each other's hands in their new habit. Bren had started seating him across the table from her, not so she couldn't hold his hand, but so she could look at him. The touch was dangerous, anyway.

Rob prayed a blessing over the food, and everyone dug in.

After the meal was over, the kitchen tidied, and the children in bed, Bren walked straight into Rob's arms.

He held her close and rested his cheek on the top of her head. "I've been thinking..."

When he didn't finish his thought, her butterflies broke formation and bounced all over her insides. "Sounds dangerous."

"I know you said you were going to Kennewick for Thanksgiving, but I've been wondering." He paused. "Would you like to come to Spokane with me instead? I'd like you to meet my family."

His family? His parents and sister, to say nothing of his fierce-sounding grandmother? His aunts, uncles... Bren shook her head before she'd finished the mental list. "No, I couldn't. It's too soon."

Rob's finger lifted her chin. "I'd been thinking that, too, but I changed my mind."

She met his gaze for a second before he lowered his mouth and kissed her thoroughly. Responding to the kiss was easier than words. She wasn't ready to tell the world how she felt about Rob Santoro. Kristen and Marisa already had a good idea, but they'd wheedled it out of her.

Meeting his family at Thanksgiving, no less, meant putting herself and her emotions on display. It meant telling her children of her hopes for the future, and risking them getting hurt. Risking *her* getting hurt with curious eyes watching. Maybe condemning eyes.

"Do you know why I changed my mind, Bren?" he whispered.

She shook her head, unwilling to talk when they could be kissing.

"Because I realized something. I realized I love you, and I want the whole world to know."

"Oh!" Had that startled sound really come from her mouth? Rob was getting off-script. Taking her out of the place that had only become a comfort zone in the past week.

"Surprised?" His voice teased gently. "Didn't you guess?"

"I-I don't know what to say."

"Can you tell me you love me, too?"

"I, um. I'm not sure what love is."

Rob's hands caressed her back, keeping her close against him, warming her. "I didn't mean to rush you. I only wanted you to know that my thoughts have gone beyond mere friendship. Beyond a simple relationship, if there's such a thing, anyway."

The friendship stage had been mighty short, but she could have done with a longer relationship stage. How could he really know, after only a month, that his feelings were deeper than that? Hadn't they been comfortable spending time together? A lot of time, she had to admit, even to herself. And, okay, it hadn't been comfortable.

She longed for more, but it terrified her at the same time. Every guy who'd ever talked about love had only meant sex. Rob was different. She knew he was different.

"What are you afraid of, sweetheart? I love you. I won't hurt you or push you. I won't take advantage of you. I promise."

See? Different. She wanted him to desire her that way, but not yet. Because once they'd gone there, he wouldn't want her anymore. The realization slammed into her like a blast of November wind. Was that why she held back? Because he'd reject her?

Was it better or worse to reject him first? She didn't want rejection. She wanted the status quo to carry on for a long, long time. While it flirted with danger, it was still a safe place.

"My friend in Kennewick is expecting me." Her voice didn't come out as strong as she'd hoped. Bren cleared her throat and tried again. "Sabrina moved away from Helena two years ago. Her kids were my kids' best friends."

Rob's hands ceased smoothing down the back of her top. He held her shoulders and waited until she looked up at him. "Is that what you truly want to do for Thanksgiving?"

Not really? Her breath caught along with her gaze. She stretched and brushed her lips across his.

He didn't respond the way she'd hoped he would. "Bren? I'd really like it if you came with me. I want my family — my old neighborhood — to see what a treasure I've found. I want them to know you and be glad with me."

"But I'm not..." No, he had an answer for that, too. He always did.

His eyes caressed hers. "They'll love you. They'll understand."

He was referring to the kids. To her imperfect past. See, he still thought about it, even though he said it didn't matter. She couldn't help stiffening. "No."

His eyes, usually so warm and inviting, held a hint of hurt. "Whatever you want, Bren."

She hadn't meant to put that pain there. Bren reached up and cradled his face, his evening stubble rough on her palms. "I'm sorry," she breathed. "I just can't."

Rob turned and pressed his lips to her right palm. "I'm sorry for pushing you." He gave her a lopsided smile. "I should get going."

She hadn't even gotten out the movie she'd thought they'd watch this evening. "Do you have to?"

"I think I do. I have to pack for the trip." He kissed her mouth lightly. "I'll talk to you later, okay?"

Bren nodded as he pulled on his leather jacket and then his boots. She'd put her foot in it this time. On the other hand, if he were so easy to dissuade, it was better to know now.

He stood with his hand on the knob for a long moment, looking deep into her eyes. "Bren, I love you, but I don't love you a fraction as much as God does."

And then he was gone.

Chapter 11

*F*rancesca tells me you have met a woman."

It was ten-thirty at night, and Rob had been in the door all of ten minutes. Long enough to use the washroom and drop his bags in his old bedroom. He looked at his mom, standing in the doorway, a hopeful expression on her face.

"Fran wasn't supposed to tell."

Mom waved a hand. "She let something drop, and I made her tell the rest."

Figured. A few days ago he'd been on cloud nine, but all last night, all day at work, and every minute of his five-hour drive he'd alternated worrying about and praying for Bren. Were they doomed? Was it too much to think he could help her claim her identity in Jesus? Would he always be the one holding her up? And if he was, was that so bad?

"Rob?"

109

"Yes, I've met someone." He knew better than to make his mother wait until morning.

Mom came in and perched on the edge of his bed. "Is she pretty? Does she love the Lord?"

"Yes to both. And I imagine Fran told you she has two children."

"Yes. Is she widowed? Divorced?"

"Neither. She just came to faith a couple of years ago."

Mom bit her lip. "Are you sure this is a wise move?"

"Did you choose to fall in love with Dad?"

"Of course not. He was so charming. So handsome. I lost my heart before I made a conscious decision, and I have not regretted it one minute of thirty-seven years."

"I didn't choose to fall in love with Bren, either."

"You are in love?" Mom's voice was hushed as her eyes searched his.

He nodded.

"But that is *magnifico*! When can we meet her? When will be the wedding?"

"Not so fast." Chuckling, Rob held up a hand. "Give me time."

"But you have had twenty-eight years. I was about to lose hope."

"Surely you didn't expect me to marry twenty years ago, Mamma?" He fell into his childhood name for her.

"No, of course not." She waved a hand. "But what are you waiting for now?"

"To be sure this is who God has for me. More than that, for Bren to be sure."

Mom looked him up and down. "What can she find to resist? You are a fine man, Roberto. Handsome like your papa and just as kind."

Rob shook his head. "Bren doesn't trust easily. She is sure everyone looks down upon her for her past. For the fact that her children have different fathers and she wasn't married to either one of them. She has become a Christian, yes, but still feels she needs to be good enough."

"Good enough for what? The blood of Jesus covers all."

"I know that, Mamma. She knows it, too. But inside herself, she struggles."

"But..."

"It's not something I can do for her. I can accept her children. I can show love to her and to them. But she must still take that leap of faith on her own."

"Tell me about her children. Two, Francesca says?"

Rob pulled out his phone, opened the photo app, and sat down beside his mom. "Here are Davy and Lila the other day at the playground."

Were those tears in Mom's eyes as she touched the screen? "So precious. And their mother?"

He swiped to the next photo, one he'd taken last weekend when they'd been out with Marisa and Jase. Bren laughed, her face glowing.

"She is lovely."

"I know. Even more beautiful on the inside."

Mom peered at the phone as though memorizing Bren's features or trying to communicate with her. "Why didn't you bring her to meet us? We have room. We would welcome her."

"I know, Mamma. She already had plans with friends for the weekend." He only hoped Bren's old car made the trip to Kennewick safely. She needed new tires. Actually, she needed a whole new vehicle, but he couldn't very well get her one. Not when she made such a big deal over the flowers.

Mom patted his arm as she rose. "I will let you get some sleep, son. Your sister's family will be here for brunch in the morning, and then we'll have turkey dinner with your nonna and everyone later. You'd best keep those photos handy. Your relatives will want to see her."

She shouldn't have come. Shouldn't have assumed her friend would want to hear about Jesus. Should have remembered Sabrina never missed a chance to host a party.

A dozen people smoked pot in Sabrina's living room, and several had left the room, hands groping each other. Davy and Lila huddled on the floor in a corner, eyes wide.

Bren didn't dare assume the room she and the kids had been assigned wasn't in use even now. This had been her life. The kids had seen it plenty of times, but not in the past three years.

"You came in from Montana for the party?"

She turned to see a guy drop onto the seat beside her and give her a once-over.

"Want a joint?" He held one toward her lips. "Or maybe something else?"

Bren pushed his hand away, cringing. "No, thanks."

God, what am I doing here?

"Aw, come on, babe."

"I said no." She surged to her feet, but where could she go? It didn't matter where, so long as it wasn't here. *I'm sorry, Jesus. So sorry.*

She made eye contact with Davy and jerked her head toward the front hall. Both kids sidled along the wall. A couple of people seemed to notice, but no one said anything.

"Mommy?" whispered Lila. "I don't like this."

"Yeah, me neither." Davy set his jaw and looked past Bren into the living room.

"Listen, you two. I made a mistake, and I'm sorry." She dug in her pocket for her car keys and handed them to Davy. "I want you to go out to the car, okay? I'll be there in a minute. I just have to get our luggage out of the bedroom and tell Sabrina we're leaving."

"Where are we going?"

Bren squeezed her daughter. "I don't know. A hotel, maybe." Not that she wanted to spend her hard-earned money on a room. "We'll make that decision once we're out, okay?"

Davy poked his sister. "Get your coat. Come on."

The guy she'd pushed away watched through the doorway.

"Lock the car doors," she said to Davy. "Only open them for me."

113

"Yeah, sure." Davy stuffed his feet into his boots.

"I'm really tired, Mommy." Lila again.

"I know, sweetie. I'll only be a minute. Promise."

Bren skirted the living room and headed down the corridor. A couple were making out on the floor in front of her room. She reached over them to push open the door then flipped on the light.

"Hey!" A guy sat up on the bed.

Bren averted her eyes. "Just getting my suitcase." She grabbed both bags and heaved them over the couple in the hallway. Man, enough was enough. When had she ever thought this was a good time?

Guilt slammed her. Not that long ago, really. Three years? Davy and Lila had been conceived on nights not unlike this.

"Leaving so soon?"

Oh, no, the guy had followed her. Now he blocked her exit as he leaned against the hallway wall.

Bren gave him a bright smile. "I sure am. This isn't my scene anymore."

"Dunno. Sabrina told me how you were always so much fun. I came here just to meet you." He waggled his eyebrows. "Thought we could get to know each other."

"I'm not interested. My kids are waiting for me, and we're leaving now."

He took a step closer. "They won't mind waiting. They're probably used to it."

"Listen, buster. I don't even know your name—"

"Dylan."

"Not that it makes any difference. I am not interested. Not even a little bit. So please move out of my way."

"C'mon, babe..."

Bren swung the strap of one bag over her shoulder and held the other in front of her with both hands. She stepped forward and rammed the suitcase into his midsection. "Please move."

His eyes hardened.

He wasn't as out of it as she'd thought. *Please, Lord. Wisdom? Strength?*

"Why'd you even come if you're going to be like this?"

Looking past Dylan, she found Sabrina in the living room straddling some guy's lap. "Sabrina and I used to be friends, but I don't live like this anymore."

"Too good for us now?"

If he only knew the depth of her guilt, but she wasn't about to go into detail. Not ever, but especially not now when her kids were sitting in a cold car unchaperoned.

"Nope, I met Jesus. You should look Him up sometime. He changes lives."

He swore under his breath. "You're a religious weirdo. Don't bother calling the cops. They don't care. Smoking weed is legal in Washington now."

"I'm aware of that, and have no plans to call the police. Just getting me and my kids out of here." She angled to edge past him. "Excuse me, please."

"I should make you..."

She lifted her chin and stared him down. "Jesus is my best friend."

Dylan's nose curled and he took a step back. "You're not even worth the trouble."

"That's where you're wrong. To Jesus, I am worth everything. He died to save me."

The man raised both hands as though to protect himself from her words. Bren pushed past him, surveyed the room, and angled toward the front door. The kids had been waiting long enough.

A few minutes later, she crawled into the sub-zero vehicle and turned the key. It took a few tries for the engine to turn over. Bren rubbed her gloves together and eyed the front door. Closed. Good.

"It will warm up in here in just a few minutes, and you guys can sleep."

"Where are we going, Mom?" asked Davy from the backseat.

What were her options? It wasn't like she wanted to see Sabrina, even tomorrow. She'd send her a text and let her know they'd left. She'd pick up the relationship pieces later if possible.

Someone stood in front of Sabrina's living room window and twitched the drapery.

They needed to get out of Kennewick in case Dylan cared enough to follow. Probably not, after he'd seemed insulted by the name of Jesus, but Bren's hands still shook.

No, she needed to get some miles down the highway. At the moment, she felt wired enough to make the entire seven-hour trip home without stopping, but that would likely wear off. They hadn't left Helena until after school, so it had been a long day already.

The door to Sabrina's house cracked open.

"Mommy?" Behind her, Lila's voice quavered.

Bren shifted the car into gear and navigated out of Sabrina's subdivision without seeing headlights in her mirrors. Whew. She passed several hotels, all with no vacancy signs, on her way to a twenty-four-hour gas station. That made the decision easier. She could always pull into a rest area for an hour-long nap if she needed to, but she'd better stick to the interstate instead of heading over Lolo Pass so late at night.

They'd drive through Spokane.

Bren squeezed the gas nozzle and watched the tally mount up, her face burning even in the cold. The operative word was through. Rob was going to have a Norman Rockwell Thanksgiving dinner tomorrow, surrounded by a large, loving family, unlike the group assembled at Sabrina's. She didn't belong in his world but, thank the Lord, she didn't belong in Sabrina's, either.

It was past midnight before the car warmed up enough to be comfortable. Davy and Lila leaned against the back doors, their afghans from a woman in the church tucked up to their chins. Bren turned a worship CD up a little louder, singing along and tapping her fingers.

At the next curve, the car didn't respond instantly to her hand on the wheel. She swallowed panic and put all her might into the turn before the vehicle shifted back into its lane. It was all but impossible to steer. What was going on?

Chapter 12

An incessant buzz forced Rob from a deep sleep. He blinked in the solid darkness. Where was he? The noise sounded again. His parents' house in Spokane. That was his phone. He reached for it and knocked it off the nightstand onto the floor. Somehow his fumbling fingers closed around it.

Why was it ringing? He squinted at the clock. One-thirty? Who would call at this time? The phone was silent in his hand, but he thumbed it on to see a missed call from Bren.

Bren?

He sat straight up in bed, fully awake. She'd texted upon her arrival in Kennewick several hours ago, as he'd asked her to do. Just as he'd texted her when he got to Spokane. So why was she calling?

Her phone rang once before she answered. "Rob? I'm sorry for waking you up."

Rob's instincts rose to high alert. He'd never heard Bren's voice sound like this. Almost... fear? "No problem, sweetheart. It's always good to hear your voice." He paused for a second. "Everything okay?"

She laughed, a forced sound. "Not really. The car broke down, and the tow truck I called won't get here for a couple of hours. There's a bad accident on the highway from Edwall they're trying to clear." Her voice caught. "I don't know what to do."

"You did the right thing, calling me." He swung his legs over the side of the bed and flipped on the lamp. "Where are you? What happened?"

"I can't steer the car. It just... froze. The last sign I passed said it was something like forty miles to Spokane."

"You're on I-90? Have you passed Sprague?"

"Uh..." Her voice went quiet for a few seconds. "I'm not sure. I don't think so."

"I'm coming."

"But..."

"Bren. I love you. You need me. I'm coming. How could it be any other way?"

She sniffled, and his heart crushed.

"The kids okay?"

"It's cold."

He had no doubt that was true. "Do you have any blankets? Get in the backseat and huddle with them. I'll call again when I'm on the road. Twenty minutes, tops."

"Okay."

When was the last time anyone had told Bren what to do, and she'd actually done it? Rob reached for his jeans, mind racing. Man, a car that wouldn't steer? Rob wasn't mechanically inclined, but his cousin knew his way around engines.

One-forty in the morning. He'd do it for Peter if the roles were reversed. He searched his contacts for Peter's number and tapped it.

"This better be good, Rob."

"Hey, I need a favor." He launched into a quick explanation, and the call ended with his cousin promising to be there in under ten minutes.

By the time Peter's pickup turned into Rob's parents' driveway, Rob had gotten dressed, grabbed a few quilts, and assembled a bag of snacks. He climbed into the warm interior and tossed everything into the backseat. "Can we stop at a gas station? I need to get a coffee for Bren and hot chocolate for the kids. They must be freezing."

Peter nodded and headed toward the interstate. "Sounds like you should pick up a quart of power steering fluid while you're at it. Then we've got half an hour or so for you to tell me the unabridged version of your story." He glanced at Rob, a grin poking at his unshaven cheeks. "I thought you were going to die an old unmarried man, like me."

"Ha. You're not dead or even as old as me. It appears that where there's life, there's hope." Rob saved the tale until he returned to the truck with a cardboard tray of hot drinks. He stashed it on the floor behind his seat, passed one of the cups to Peter, and took a sip out of his.

"Thanks, cuz." Peter set his in the cup holder and began driving. "So, about this damsel in distress. If I'm going to be a knight in shining armor, I think I deserve to hear the whole story of how an avowed bachelor of twenty-eight finds himself embroiled with a woman with two kids."

If he was ready to tell anyone everything, it was Peter.

⁓ ⌒ ⌒

Bren lay awake, staring at the ceiling of Rob's childhood bedroom, Lila snuggled against her side. This wasn't how she'd planned her weekend. Not at all.

Maybe that was the problem. She'd done the planning, as usual. She'd envisioned sitting at Sabrina's kitchen table, sharing Jesus with her. Would that ever happen now that she'd run? Yet, what else could she have done?

Rob. Always there for her, no questions asked. That he'd get up in the middle of the night and come for her, along with his cousin, still amazed her. It was past four o'clock by the time they'd pulled in at Rob's parents' house. He'd shown her and Lila to his bedroom, carried Davy to the loveseat in the family room, and claimed the sofa for his own bed for what remained of the night.

His parents were going to freak out when they got up in the morning and discovered they had uninvited company. Weren't they? But if they were half as nice as Peter — half as nice as Rob — it would be okay.

This isn't what I planned, Lord.

How had she thought to meet his parents? Have them visit Helena, where she could make a nice dinner from the farm's offerings? Come to Spokane some other time with Rob, arriving fresh and prepared at a reasonable hour?

Truth? Her mind had veered away from meeting his family. She'd tried to convince herself that she and Rob were just friends. The kissing had kiboshed that thought. *Just friends* didn't kiss like their very lives depended on it.

A car drove past the Santoro house, its headlights creating a wave of light cascading along the wall before leaving the bedroom in darkness again. That's what she'd convinced herself she was to Rob. A temporary ray of light. A passing fancy. One day, probably soon, he'd meet a lovely Christian woman with an untarnished past, fall in love, and whisk her off to the altar.

And Bren would carry on raising Davy and Lila by herself. Running Hiller Farm. Being self-sufficient.

Just about done feeling sorry for yourself, girl?

Bren sniffled. She was safe and warm. What she really needed was sleep, so she'd be able to read people in the morning. She thought of Davy and knew that, someday, she'd want a better woman for him than his mother had been. There'd be no way Mrs. Santoro would welcome her with open arms, regardless of what Rob said.

Rob, who'd pulled her into his arms and kissed her a few hours ago. Who'd carried one sleepy child at a time from the freezing car to the heated truck. Who'd kissed Bren again and helped her into the truck, too, before offering them all homemade muffins and a hot chocolate. Who'd stood in the subzero temperatures holding a flashlight under the hood for his cousin until the old car had started again. Who'd called to cancel the tow truck and driven Peter's truck into the city while his cousin drove hers. Who'd listened to her tale of fleeing Kennewick and assured her she'd made the right choice, that she was safe now.

That Rob.

How could she think he'd move on to a new relationship any minute? How many more ways could he prove his love to her? What was she waiting for, fireworks?

Bren rolled over and buried her face in Rob's pillow. It even smelled faintly of him.

She'd have to worry about tomorrow when it came.

"Mommy, I need to use the washroom."

Bren groaned. "It's just across the hall."

"I don't want to go by myself."

Of course she didn't. Bren couldn't blame her daughter. She didn't want to leave the relative safety of this confined space, either. Not on three hours of restless sleep and no shower. Maybe not ever. She peered at the mirror above the dresser. Yep, she looked as horrible as she felt.

"Just a sec." She dragged her purse closer and pulled out a hairbrush.

Lila put her hands over her head. "No, mommy. That brush hurts."

Bren rolled her eyes and brushed out her own hair then grabbed her robe out of her suitcase and pulled it on over her flannel jammies. "Okay, let's go." No one intercepted them as they crossed the hall, and Bren dared breathe.

They weren't so lucky on the return trip. A middle-aged woman with a crisp bob waved at them from the kitchen at the end of the corridor. "Good morning! You must be Bren. I'm Rob's mother, Genevera. We are so happy you could join us."

So much for the fleeting thought she could escape this house before anyone noticed her presence. "Um, yes. I'm Bren, and this is my daughter, Lila. My son is here somewhere." Bren should have insisted he sleep on the floor in her room. Rob's room. Never mind.

"Davy." Genevera's smile reached her eyes. "He has gone out with Rob for a few minutes. A nice young man."

At least it seemed her son had remembered some manners... and that Rob didn't need to see her looking such a mess. So far, so good. "Is it all right if I have a shower?"

"Yes, go ahead. Let me get you a towel." Genevera bustled past Bren then turned back. "Here you go." She held out her hand to Lila. "Would you like something to eat?"

Oh. Bren hadn't thought far enough to realize it would leave her daughter alone with Rob's mother.

Lila took Genevera's hand and smiled up shyly. "You're Rob's mommy?"

"I am. Come. Let's leave your mamma to her shower, okay?"

Bren blinked. Well, that had gone well. She took the shortest shower of her life then wasted the time she'd gained on her makeup and hair before venturing out into the kitchen.

Lila sat beyond Rob at the island with Davy leaning on the other end. Rob looked up and met Bren's gaze with a slow smile, reaching his hand toward her.

She moved closer as though magnetically drawn until she stood in the circle of Rob's arm. He tugged her to his knee and kissed her. Right there in front of her kids. She looked up and felt the flush shoot up her cheeks. In front of his parents.

Genevera smiled indulgently while a man with gray-streaked hair reached out to shake her hand. "Be welcome here, Bren. I'm Frank."

"Pleased to meet you. This is a lovely house you have here." *Shut up, Bren. Don't start babbling.*

"Thank you." Genevera reached for the coffee pot. "Would you like a cup?"

"Yes, please. Just black."

Rob nuzzled her neck. "I should warn you—"

"Hello? Where is everybody? I see a car out front! Who's here?"

Bren stiffened at the woman's voice from the front entry, but Rob didn't release her. Instead he kissed her cheek before calling out a welcome. "In the kitchen, Fran. Come meet Bren."

"Bren? You brought her after all? Oh, Rob, I told you and told you and you finally listened to me." The voice grew louder and then a woman of about thirty hurried through the archway, holding a toddler. She wrapped one arm around Bren. "I'm Rob's big sister Fran and this is my little guy Luca." Fran glanced back to the entry. "Tad!

Come meet Bren. And look, two lovely children. You must be Lila." She pinched Lila's cheek. "And Davy."

Davy ducked away, and Fran laughed, the sound filling the kitchen. A girl a bit younger than Lila ran into the room and was scooped up by Genevera. Then Tad arrived, nodding and shaking Bren's hand while Fran continued to talk.

Bren had lost track of what Rob's sister was saying.

Rob leaned closer. "Yes, she's always like this," he whispered. "She bossed me around ever since I was born. You could say she made me the man I am today."

Bren turned toward him, their faces only inches apart. "Then I'm sure I'll love her."

Rob swept his lips over hers. "Good girl. It will be mutual."

"So, Lila, have you finished that cinnamon bun?" Genevera set her granddaughter down and reached for the toddler. "Maybe you'd like to go play with Tieri? She can show you the toys. Tieri is five."

The two little girls eyed each other then Lila nodded, slid off, and followed the younger girl out of the room.

"So, that's the little girl who's going to be in a beauty pageant?" Fran said from across the island.

Bren froze. She hadn't even brushed Lila's hair yet, and Lila had insisted on bringing her tattered pajamas that were nearly too small on this trip.

Rob's hand tightened around Bren. "Yep, that's the one."

Chapter 13

ren's fingers tightened around Rob's, and he squeezed back. "Wow," she murmured, looking around.

He could just imagine how all this could overwhelm her. Good grief, the crowd overwhelmed him, and he was related to every one of the thirty-some people in the community center, the vast majority by blood, and a few by marriage. His cousins' marriages, that is.

"The architecture is amazing. I love how they've restored this brick building."

Rob shook his head. She was awed by the building, not the teeming mass of Santoros it held? "Uh, yeah. Fran told me they've been at this renovation for months. Used to be a retail store selling paintings and sculptures, but it's been empty for quite a few years."

"Come." Tieri held out her hand to Lila on the other side of Bren, and the two of them headed off to a corner where Rob's cousin's two little kids had a floor puzzle going on.

Davy still stood beside Rob.

Nearby, Fran clapped her hands and yelled for attention. "Everyone, I want you to meet Rob's girlfriend, Bren, from Helena! And her kids, Davy and Lila." She turned to him and Bren. "I'd give you everyone's names, but I suspect you'd forget them after the first one."

Bren nodded, offering a little smile and wave to the group, who'd all paused to stare at her.

"Roberto! You did not tell me you were seeing a woman!"

Rob cringed as everyone parted, allowing his grandmother a direct path. "Here she comes," he whispered to Bren. Then he took a few steps, pulling her along. "Hi, Nonna. Happy Thanksgiving." He kissed her cheek while her hands grasped both sides of his face with surprising strength.

"Look at you. You are thin. Are you eating well? What kind of food do they have in Montana? You take some salami and jars of marinara back with you, *si*? Or maybe you will return to the bosom of your family soon."

"I'm doing well, Nonna. I have a good job in Helena, and I like it there. Bren is a farmer. I think you'd be impressed by all the canning in her pantry. She's a very good cook."

Nonna turned to Bren and studied her for a long moment. "A farmer?"

"Pleased to meet you, Mrs. Santor—"

"Marietta."

Bren nodded in acknowledgment. "Yes, I manage Hiller Farm, which supplies a good amount of produce to Helena's largest community-supported agriculture box program."

Nonna opened her mouth and closed it again.

Rob bit back a grin. It wasn't often anyone impressed his grandmother enough to halt the flow of words. It didn't last long.

"You have children? What of their father?"

Bren's hand tightened in his convulsively. "Not in the picture."

"Ah, but—"

Time to end the interrogation. "Say, Nonna. That turkey smells good. Did you brine it the way you used to?" He turned to Bren. "She always tossed a bunch of oranges and lemons in. So good."

Nonna looked between him and Bren. "Yes, there is a citrus brine."

"Mamma!" called Rob's aunt from the kitchen. "Can you come make the gravy? Everything is nearly ready to go out."

Rob grinned at his grandmother's indecision. "We can visit more later. Is there anything Bren and I can do to help?"

The long tables had already been set with plain white plates and gleaming silverware. A metal folding chair was pulled up in front of each place. Several of his teen girl cousins made the rounds, adding a napkin to each setting.

"Make yourself at home," Nonna said at last, turning for the kitchen.

"She's something else," Bren whispered against his sleeve.

"Don't let her get to you. You did great."

"That's your grandmother?" asked Davy. "She's scary."

Rob set his hand on the boy's shoulder. "She's the boss, all right. Everybody knows it."

A chuckle made him glance up to see his cousin approaching. "She's not as tough as she sounds. Hi, I'm Jasmine. Nice to meet you, Bren. And you are...?" She held out her hand to Davy.

The boy glanced up at Rob before taking Jasmine's hand. "I'm Davy."

Jasmine glanced around. "Michael is here somewhere. I think he's about your age. Maybe after dinner, you can go outside with him. The playground is just across the street."

Davy nodded. "Maybe."

"You know why Nonna is upset with you?" Jasmine had a conspiratorial twinkle in her eye as she glanced between them.

"Uh... she's upset? She seemed normal."

Jasmine tossed her head back and laughed. "She's upset because Eden Andrusek is engaged. To some other man, obviously."

Rob groaned. "She can't still have thought Eden and I were going to get together? I dated her what, once, in high school?"

"You know Nonna. She doesn't give up easily. Eden's guy is really nice, though. I'm happy for her."

"That's great. I wish her well." When was the last time he'd even thought of the girl who'd attracted him briefly more than ten years ago? He disentangled his hand from Bren's and wrapped his arm around her instead. "I'm pretty happy with the way things turned out, myself. Nonna will just have to get used to it."

Jasmine grinned at Bren. "I can't wait to get to know you. Rob spent so much time at our house when we were all growing up, he almost seemed like one of my brothers. When you already have four of them, what's one more?"

"Four brothers?" asked Bren. "I can't even imagine."

His cousin leaned in. "It's a lot of testosterone, let me tell you. They broke more than one lamp while wrestling. Mamma kicked the whole lot of them outside the house more times than anyone could count."

Good memories. Well, except for the broken lamp he'd personally been responsible for, but that had been from basketball, not wrestling. "The guys still play three-on-three?"

Jasmine's eyes brightened. "Yeah, they do. Peter and Basil still miss you, too. So much they had to drag a non-Santoro onto their team."

He chuckled. "Desperation. Surely there's a cousin or two still available?"

"Marco quit playing. Says he's too busy with his kids. And the younger guys have a team or two of their own." She turned to Bren. "We take three-on-three very seriously. Spokane has a competition called Hoopfest every year in June, and our boys usually do very well."

Bren looked up at him. "Do you still play?"

He shook his head. "Not really. Not since I moved away. Basketball's a team sport, and I—"

She laughed. "And you prefer solo things, like hiking and cycling. I get it."

"Did you ever play sports?" He knew her high school years had been cut short, but maybe before that?

"Some." She shrugged, biting her lip.

Rob caressed her shoulder.

"We'll probably all get out and shoot some hoops later," said Jasmine. "There's a whole lot less dishes to do having a family dinner here at the community center with its shiny commercial dishwasher. Probably our moms will kick us out once the leftovers are packed away."

He glanced down at Bren. "Want to? You don't have to."

She looked up at him, eyebrows rising. "You're on."

༄ ‿ ༄

That hadn't been so bad. Not so different from a church dinner back in Helena, really, except here everyone was related. Other than her and her kids, but after Marietta's few pointed questions, no one had made a big deal of them being there. They'd even been friendly. Rob's aunts had introduced themselves. The teen girls had smiled shyly at her as they filled serving bowls. The younger boys had ignored her, focusing instead on Davy, while the older guys had introduced themselves then slapped Rob's back and started in on guy talk. There didn't seem to be many girl cousins in their twenties.

The group laughed, talked, and headed across the street to the basketball courts. The gray November day was already darkening, but the courts were well lit from lights under the bridge that sheltered them.

Bren glanced around. Davy hung upside down from the monkey bars with other boys nearby. Fran had said Lila would be fine inside with Tieri and the others. Could Bren really jump in and play basketball with the guys? She had to, now. Rob had made a quick trip back to the house for their sneakers, so she had no excuse.

Jasmine tossed the ball at her. Man, it had been eons since she'd played. Bren eyed the basket, dribbled closer, and set up a shot. It bounced off the backboard.

Rob whistled. "That was pretty close for someone who hasn't played in ten years."

He had the timing pegged about right. Everything had changed when she'd gotten pregnant with Davy. First all the puking and the exhaustion. Then her junior year was over and she hadn't bothered going back. Her friends were doing the same things they always had. Classes, sports, dances, parties by the river. Their lives had gone on. Hers had taken a sudden swing into left field. The guy she'd slept with had told her to get an abortion. So had her mom, but somehow she couldn't follow through.

So maybe Rob's grandmother didn't think Bren was good enough for a Santoro. The old lady hadn't quite said so, but with that scowl, what else could she have been thinking? She'd already had somebody picked out for Rob.

"Want to start, or take Jasmine's place in a few minutes?" Rob bounced the ball on the concrete pad in front of her.

Peter and a guy they called Basil stretched their hamstrings.

"Maybe I'll just watch."

Rob shot the ball at her. She caught it instinctively and shot it back.

"Not a chance, sweetheart. You, me, and Peter will start." He turned to the guys. "Who are we up against?"

"Alex's team."

"Bring it."

Had Rob always been this bossy? He dribbled in a low, tight, circle then jumped, arching the ball toward the hoop.

Swish.

Peter caught the ball and fired it at her.

Guess she was playing now.

A few minutes later, Basil came in for her, and she sagged beside Jasmine at the picnic table. "Wow, it's been ages."

Jasmine grinned but kept watching the play. "Way to hold your own."

"I didn't even score a point. And we're losing."

"You blocked some shots. These guys are intense. They keep forgetting it's all in good fun." She bounced to her feet. "I'm going in for Rob."

Rob dropped down beside Bren and slung his arm around her. "You did good."

"Thanks." She watched as Alex's team got another basket. "I need to use the washroom. Be right back."

"Sure. Right by the door to the kitchen. Hurry back. We need you." He dropped a kiss to her hair.

Bren laughed as she crossed the street. They needed her as much as they needed weights around their ankles. She entered the community center, catching a glimpse of Lila and her new friends coloring at a table on the far side. A minute later she came out of the washroom to hear voices in the nearby kitchen.

"You are going to turn out just like Rob's girlfriend."

Bren stopped in mid-step. Was that Rob's grandmother? Sure sounded like her.

"She seems nice."

One of the teen girls. Bren couldn't remember any of their names, but thanks to this one for sticking up for her.

Marietta clucked. "You watch yourself with that boy, Dafne. Fran tells me that woman didn't even finish high school because she was pregnant. Don't end up like her."

That woman? Bren took a step closer.

"I'm—"

"Mark my words, child. Follow Jesus and be smart. Get your degree and then get married. I want more great-grandchildren, *si*, but not like that."

Not like Bren? Or not from a teenaged Dafne?

Half of her wanted to march into that kitchen and face them. Yeah, she didn't want Rob's cousin to be a teen mom, either, but she could hold her head up and speak of God's mercy and redemption.

"Nonna, I—"

"Be a good girl, Dafne. Yes, God forgives, but the stain remains."

The impulse to confront Rob's grandmother withered. Yes, this was what Bren kept telling Rob. How could he not understand? How could he treat Davy and Lila so well, like maybe they were his? He knew the circumstances of their conceptions wasn't the kids' fault.

No, it was hers. Hers and those boys she'd given herself to as a teenager. The boys that had absolved themselves of all responsibility years ago, leaving her holding the bag all by herself.

Her chin came up. Well, she'd managed just fine, thank you. At least once she'd met Jesus.

But Rob's nonna was right. The stain remained.

Chapter 14

Rob glanced up when Bren entered the kitchen the next morning, her face red and puffy. She didn't look like she'd slept at all but, whatever the problem was, it had started last night. When she came back to the basketball court, she'd refused to play again. Soon enough he'd made their excuses to the cousins and taken Bren back to his parents' house, where she'd disappeared into his old bedroom.

"Good morning, Bren." He held out his hand for her, but she headed to the coffee pot instead and poured a cup.

"Morning." She looked around. "Where are the kids?"

"In the rec room. Tieri's here. Did you sleep well?"

Bren shrugged. "Okay, I guess. I'm really thankful for your rescue, but I need to head back to Helena today. The car's good, right?"

What *had* happened inside the community center last night? Bren had yet to meet his gaze since. Rob swung off

139

the stool, rounded the island, and gathered her in his arms. While she didn't exactly resist him, she didn't return the hug.

Rob tipped her face up and kissed her. "I love you," he whispered. "What's your hurry? You'd planned to spend the entire weekend in Kennewick, hadn't you?"

She let out a shaky breath. "Yeah."

"So stay. Please?"

"I... I don't fit here. This isn't my normal."

He rubbed her back, resting his cheek on the top of her head. "It could be." His hands stilled. What had he just said? Offering her this lifestyle, his family, was halfway to a proposal.

Bren pushed away far enough to look up at him. "Rob. Don't."

"Don't what?" He brushed a kiss over her mouth.

"Don't go there." Her breath was ragged. "I really need to go home. This whole weekend has just been too much, what with Sabrina's party." She looked away. "Your family. Everything."

"What happened last night?"

She ducked under his arm and lifted her coffee cup with trembling fingers. "It doesn't matter."

"It looks like it does."

Bren shook her head. "My car is drivable, right? It only needed that quart of oil or whatever? I should pay Peter for his time. Getting up in the middle of the night like that. And you..."

"Bren."

"What?"

"Two things, okay?" He ached to hold her, but as he reached for her, she sidled out of easy reach. "One, you do not owe Peter anything. He's my cousin. He was happy to help. And you definitely don't owe me anything. Don't you understand? I love you. When you love someone, you're there for them when they need it. You don't count the cost or a couple of hours of missed sleep. All that matters is the one you love."

Did she love him that way? Rob's heart clenched as he watched her staring into her coffee cup. Would she *ever* love him that way, or was she too hung up on her past?

"The second thing?"

Rob closed his eyes for a second, absorbing the blow that she hadn't responded to his declaration. She'd brushed it aside. Brushed *him* aside.

"I took your car down to a used car lot this morning."

"You *what*?" Right, *now* he had all her attention.

"A guy I knew in school runs it. Dan Ranta. I wanted him to have a look, because he knows older vehicles. He has a pretty good idea how much life a car has left in it. What it's worth."

Bren raised her eyebrows. "And?"

"It's not looking good. He says the reason the fluid leaked out is that the steering gear box is completely shot. I had to add another quart to get it back to the house."

"Let me guess. For five hundred dollars, he can fix it and it will be as good as new." Skepticism tinged her words.

"More than that, actually." Rob pushed off the counter and tried to take Bren's cup from her, but she wouldn't let go. How could he hold her with near-boiling coffee between them? Maybe that was her point.

Was he losing her? His heart sank. He'd known it was too early to bring her to meet his family, but circumstances had conspired against him. Or was it God? It had to be God. Maybe the Almighty was showing him, here and now, that there wasn't a future with Bren Haddock.

Rob couldn't accept that. *Wouldn't* accept it. Not even if it were really God's will to let her go? His head felt squeezed in a vice. *God, I need some clear direction. I need Your wisdom.*

I have loved you with an everlasting love.

Bren sighed. "So you're telling me I'm stranded here."

"Do you have a mechanic you can trust in Helena?"

She shook her head. "No. I've been going on a wing and a prayer with that car for quite a while now. I knew something would happen sometime, but..."

"But newer cars cost a lot."

"I've saved some." She eyed him. "I wanted to put it off as long as possible."

"Sounds like you're at that point." How much was *some*? Rob longed to buy her a car. She wouldn't accept it, and the offer would make a promise she wasn't ready to hear. "Want me to give Dan a call? We can go down and see what he has on the lot. Sounded like he might be shutting down, so he might have some deals."

"Going out of business?"

"Going into a different business. Not because he hasn't made a go of this one."

"You trust him?"

Rob shrugged. "I don't know him well, but he didn't try to sell me a vehicle on the spot. Just answered my questions about what's up with yours."

⌒‿ℓ‿ɕ

Bren hated draining her savings account for a car, but what choice did she have? She'd socked away a bit every month since coming on board at Hiller Farm. She'd signed a contract for another year, so she'd be able to make the payments. Wouldn't she?

She followed Rob back to his parents' Bridgeview neighborhood in a new-to-her car and parked it along the street. With winter coming, just the fact that the tires had lots of tread was worth a portion of the sale. She got out of the car and examined the deep, foreboding gray sky that smelled of snow.

Davy came running out the door, Michael at his heels. "Is that our new car? Suh-weet!"

"Yeah." Bren glanced at Rob walking toward them from where he'd parked. She turned back to her son and lowered her voice. "Tell Lila to get ready. I think we'll head for Helena before that storm rolls in."

"But, Mom! I don't want to. Michael has this cool space game, and I'm just getting the hang of it."

"Davy."

Rob stepped up beside her. "What's up?"

"Mom wants to go home now." Davy scowled and kicked at a clump of dry grass.

"Bren—"

"Don't," she whispered.

A few lazy snowflakes fluttered past her, one landing on her sleeve. No.

"It's supposed to snow all evening and night then clear off. Better to sit tight."

She hated his logic. Hated him. No, she didn't. She'd love him given half a chance. She needed to leave Spokane before she had to face his grandmother again. Before Rob realized the woman was right, that Bren's stain would always remain. She couldn't let him give up his own clean slate for her. He'd thank her later.

His arm slipped around her as the boys scampered inside, shouting about a snowstorm. "Let's go for a walk, okay? We need to talk."

It didn't sound like a question or even a suggestion. It was the next best thing to an order. "Rob, I—"

"Sweetheart, I need to know what happened to take the sunshine from your face."

She yanked out of his grasp. "Rob, it's better this way. It really is." If only she could trust him. Trust his words. But she couldn't. It was all up to her. Always had been, always would be. "Thank you for helping me with the car, but I can't stay."

The sadness and confusion on his face nearly undid her, but she was nothing if not strong. She turned before she did something foolish, like reach for him. Kiss him. She hurried up the sidewalk to light a fire under her kids. It was only three o'clock. They could be home by eight or nine. Marisa wouldn't have to come out to the farm for the rest of the weekend to gather eggs.

"Lila! Davy! Get your things together." She angled straight for Rob's bedroom and threw her clothes into her suitcase. Stuffed Lila's belongings into the other bag. Glanced around the room to make sure she hadn't left anything.

Rob would be happy to sleep in his bed after two nights on the sofa.

She hauled the luggage to the front door. Where were the kids, anyway? First things first. She loaded the car, admiring the roomy trunk, then returned to the house. In the basement, she found Davy and Michael playing a computer game while Lila and Tieri strutted around in vintage gowns, high heels, and flamboyant hats.

"Davy! Lila! I told you to get ready. Now come on."

Lila's lower lip quivered.

"Mom..." Davy whined.

Bren bit off her words. "You heard me."

Davy took one look at her face, and his eyes widened. "Coming, Mom. I'll beat you next time, Michael. Thanks."

Nice he remembered his manners. "Lila."

Lila kicked the heels into the corner and cast her a stink-eye. At least she did as she was told. A minute later Bren shepherded both kids up the stairs and into the front hall. "I have all your stuff. Coats and boots now."

Genevera bustled out of the kitchen. "Oh, no! What's happening? I have baked ziti ready for the oven. I was sure you'd love it."

Bren bit her lip and turned to face Rob's mom. Rob leaned in the kitchen archway beyond, looking lost. That made two of them. She was lost, too. *And stained*, she reminded herself.

"I'm sorry, Genevera. I'm sure your ziti is very good, but if I leave now, I can stay ahead of that storm."

"But stay. At least until morning, and let the crews clear the interstate before you go so far."

"They take good care of it. I'll be fine." She mustered a smile. "Thanks for everything."

She urged the kids down the sidewalk, sure that any second Rob would be standing there, holding her keys just out of reach. Catching her around the waist and kissing her soundly. But nothing happened until she'd started the car with trembling fingers.

Then her phone rang. She eyed it. Rob's number.

He'd just keep trying, wouldn't he? Maybe not.

Snow drifted by her car window at a more acute angle. A bit of wind behind that, now.

It rang again. She grabbed it up. "Hello."

"I love you, Bren. Please text me when you get in, and I'll pick you up for breakfast on Tuesday, okay?"

She swallowed the mountain in her throat. How could they just pick up where they'd left off? They couldn't. But maybe three days would give her enough time and distance to explain things so he'd understand. "Okay."

"Drive safely." And then the phone clicked off.

Bren dropped her cell like she'd been stung and turned to the backseat. "Buckled in? Let's go."

Two pairs of reproachful eyes stared back at her. Just more proof she couldn't do anything right.

Chapter 15

"Hey, what are you doing here on a Tuesday morning?" Todd leaned against the doorway of Rob's office.

Good to know the gossip mill wasn't running with the news. Rob looked up. "Bren canceled." By text then didn't respond to his next messages or his phone calls or his voicemails or his emails.

Todd's head tilted slightly as he examined Rob. "Did something happen?"

Rob had looked in the mirror that morning, and the lack of sleep from the last few nights had fully caught up to him. There was no hiding the mess. "You could say so, only I have no idea what."

His boss hip-checked the door closed and dropped into the client chair. "Tell me."

"There's not much to tell." Rob searched for hidden meanings behind everything that had happened as he gave Todd the short version. Not that there was a long version.

"Something happened in the community center?"

"Maybe." It had to have. "She won't say."

"Hmm." Todd steepled his fingers and frowned. "Want me to ask Kristen if she knows anything? I'm sure she'd have said, though, unless she was asked to keep it in confidence."

Rob shook his head. "Up to you, but I'd rather have your prayers." He could just imagine Bren's defenses rising if their mutual friends got involved.

"You definitely have those. Let's pray together right now." Todd grinned. "And while we're on the topic, I'd love to have you come to the men's prayer breakfast at church on Fridays. I won't deny six o'clock is early, but it's a powerful time."

The weekend with his extended family had reminded Rob how much fellowship he was missing by only going to Sunday morning services. Introvert or not, he needed some deeper connections. Men to walk with in faith and prayer. "I might take you up on that."

Todd nodded then launched into a heartfelt plea for God's guidance in Rob and Bren's relationship.

Rob's throat choked as he listened, making it difficult to add his own few words at the end. Yeah, he definitely needed a network.

After Todd left, Rob stared at Bren's photo on his phone for a few minutes, praying for her. He'd asked God a lot of *why* in the past few days, just as his parents and sister had asked him when Bren had run. *Why? What happened?*

He'd felt like a fool trying to explain something he had no clue of. How could he make his family understand he wasn't good enough for Bren, somehow, when she'd kept insisting she wasn't good enough for him? He'd felt like a little kid. Exposed. Vulnerable.

Davy's and Lila's eyes had reflected the same confusion and hurt. Man, he missed those kids. He'd promised to take Davy backpacking in the summer. Would Bren still let him do that? And Lila had promised to teach him how to make snow angels, but first there had to be snow.

As of this week, there *was* snow. Over a foot of it had come down over the weekend, which was no guarantee it was going to be a white Christmas.

Rob's computer pinged with an incoming message. He shook the mouse to activate the screen.

The annual Hiller Farm Sledding Party will be held this Saturday from ten until four out at the farm. Hope you're planning to attend. Todd.

Rob's spirits rose then fell.

Bren had regaled him of stories of previous winter parties. Of sledding, snowmen, cocoa, and gingerbread cookies. Of bonfires, friends, and laughter. The event was a highlight of her winter, and she wasn't talking to him. She wouldn't be impressed if he showed up.

On the other hand, she didn't own Hiller Farm. The party was put on by Marisa and her mom, and Marisa's soon-to-be brother-in-law had invited Rob.

Besides, how else was he supposed to see her? How else toboggan with Davy, or take Lila up on her offer to teach him to make snow angels?

He'd go. And not only that, he'd send a bouquet today. He'd brought flowers at least once a week since they'd met. She might be pushing him away, but he wasn't giving up hope. Not yet.

After making the call to The Floral Cottage, he opened his task list. Right at the top was managing the next part of the pageant advertising.

No, he wasn't done with Bren. She couldn't ignore him forever.

⁂

"Heather Francis is going to take over coaching the little girls." Marisa lifted her coffee cup in the Hiller Farm kitchen. "I thought I could handle it all *and* prepare to hand off the snowflake tiara on Christmas Eve *and* plan a wedding."

Bren managed a chuckle. "You're not superwoman after all?"

"Never pretended to be."

"You give off that vibe. Always together. Always poised."

"A lot of that is training." Marisa eyed Bren over the table. "It doesn't mean I can always pull it off. It doesn't mean I don't have doubts of my own."

Marisa? Doubts? Bren couldn't stop her eyebrows from arching. "Name one thing you doubt."

"I could give you ten easily. One, can I be the wife Jase needs and deserves? Two, can I give up everything I've ever known and learn how to work with him creating documentaries?" Marisa held up both hands and turned them. "These hands know how to wear nail extensions and model rings for ads. They know how to pull weeds and pit cherries."

"With gloves on."

At the moment, Marisa only wore her engagement ring with diamonds in the shape of a snowflake. It was stunningly gorgeous. Bren had barely begun to dream of a love like Marisa and Jase's with Rob before she'd cut him out of her life.

"Always with gloves. And now these hands need to learn new tasks." Marisa grinned. "My brain, too. Working with Jase creating documentaries will be a whole new experience. Being married."

Impulsively, Bren reached out and grasped one of Marisa's hands. "I'm so happy for you. You're up for the challenges."

"I hope so. I don't want to mess anything up. Do you know what the stats on marriage are these days?"

"More people stay married than get divorced. And you guys love each other. You've known each other for, what, five years? You'll be fine."

"Not quite that long, but yeah. Almost four, including the world's longest, most stressful engagement. It's been a rough year."

Marisa's idea of a rough year and Bren's were likely to be quite different, but Marisa didn't mean poverty-level rough, where Bren had been not that long ago. "I'm sure some people have been engaged for more than a year and lived through it."

"Well, I don't recommend it. I might even recommend eloping, at this stage." Marisa's eyes seemed to see right into Bren's soul. "How about it? If I'm not on my honeymoon, the kids can stay with me — with us — for a week or so."

Bren pulled her gaze away and focused on her nearly empty coffee cup. She surged to her feet and reached for the pot.

"Bren."

With her back to Marisa, her hand stilled. "Hmm? Want a refill?"

"No. I've had enough caffeine to jitter me through the day already. I have no idea how you can consume five or six cups and still function."

Bren filled her mug, trying to think of something to do that would prevent her from sitting back down and hearing Marisa's inevitable questions. Aha. "You said Heather would be taking over? She finaled in the Miss Snowflake last year, didn't she?"

"Third runner-up. She's more than qualified to coach. Kristen is talking about hiring her to handle the entire pageant portfolio next year."

"Oh, that's great. I'm sure Lila will miss you, though." Bren dared turn toward the table as she leaned against the counter.

"I'll still be around. Come sit down. Please."

There was no getting out of this. Bren lowered herself into the chair, mind still scrambling. "Doesn't Heather work for Habitat for Humanity?"

"Yes. Bren, why did you come back early from Thanksgiving? At first I thought you'd simply realized that Sabrina and you didn't have much in common anymore, but then you said something about Spokane. Did you see Rob?"

Busted. "Um, yeah. I saw him. He helped me get a good deal on the car." He'd also rescued her in the middle of the night, introduced her to his family, and made her dream — for just a little while — that her life could be so much more. That his love could endure.

"Didn't he want you to stay? I thought you said he'd invited you home to meet his family."

Bren blew the steam off her coffee. Not that it lasted. An instant later it rose just as though she hadn't done it. Nothing lasted. Didn't the Bible even say mankind was like a flower that perished in the heat? Here today; gone tomorrow. If that was the case, how could any man's love last longer? When Rob met someone else without her kind of baggage, he'd be glad to be free.

He would.

"Bren? Talk to me."

"I couldn't stay. It was all just too much." She could feel Marisa's eyes on her, but no way was she looking up.

"What happened?"

"Nothing, okay? It just wasn't meant to be."

"You decided you weren't good enough?" Her friend's voice was so soft it somehow wiggled past the barriers Bren had set.

Bren tried for a nonchalant shrug. "I've always known that, but it's been confirmed."

"By Rob?" Marisa's voice rose.

"Look, I really don't want to talk about this."

"I think you need to. Unless you've confided in someone else and have gotten it all off your chest."

Bren shook her head. "Don't worry about me, okay?"

"Why?" Marisa leaned closer, making it harder to avoid her gaze. "Because you're not worth it?"

Silence stretched. Tears threatened to pour out, but Bren blinked them back. "Seriously. Don't worry."

"You're my sister in Christ, Bren. You're someone God has brought my way to do life with. We're friends, and friends talk. They don't bottle things up and pretend everything is all right when they very obviously are not."

Bren surged to her feet and turned away. "So I'm a failure at being a friend, too."

"Oh, honey. That's not what I said and definitely not what I meant. I'm here for you. I want to help."

"No one can help. Not even God. My past is still what it is, no matter what I do in the present. Nothing helps. Okay? Nothing."

"Did Rob change his mind and decide your past mattered? Because if he did, you're right. He's not worth the effort."

She couldn't answer. Not when any second she'd lose control and burst out bawling like a baby.

Marisa's arms came around her. "I'm so sorry you're hurting. I just want to fix everything. How can I help?"

Bren stiffened. "You can't."

Marisa's hands rubbed Bren's shoulders. "Dear Lord, I bring my friend and sister Bren to you. I ask that You'd show her how very much she is loved and treasured. That You'd show her what purpose her life has as a believer. Jesus, show her Your love. Please. In Your name, amen."

"There is no purpose." Great. The words came out interspersed with sobs.

"You're wrong, Bren. God is in control. Romans eight twenty-eight, remember? God works out all things for our good. The people Paul is talking about in that verse are believers. The ones called according to God's purpose. That's you. Me. Every Christian."

The words sounded correct, but...

The doorbell rang. Baxter stumbled to his feet, barking.

Bren wiped her face, no doubt blotchy.

"Want me to see who's there?"

"Thanks. I don't want to talk to anyone."

Marisa chuckled and gave her one last squeeze. "I kind of noticed that." Her footsteps faded.

Bren blew her nose and listened for the sound of voices. All she heard was Marisa's pleasant, "Thank you so much. She'll love them."

The footsteps returned, and Bren glanced at the doorway to see a huge bouquet of roses. There must have been two dozen red blooms with baby's breath and ferns mixed in.

Rob. No one else would do this. She bit her lip.

Marisa set the display in the center of the kitchen table. "That's quite lovely, don't you think?"

No answer required.

"Evidence says that Rob loves you and hasn't given up hope you'll return the sentiment. Am I reading this correctly?"

Bren chewed her lip. The fragrance filled the space, reminding her of every word Rob had spoken to her. Every hug, kiss, and embrace. The warmth of his eyes when he looked at her. Everything they'd shared in the past month.

Marisa stood right in front of her. There was no avoiding eye contact anymore. Her friend's gaze was full of sympathy... and questions.

She'd never wanted pity. She was tough. She'd come out of a bad situation and pulled herself up by her own bootstraps. Sure, meeting Marisa and then Jesus had made a huge, huge difference, but she was only trying to be realistic. That was all.

"Don't you want to see the card?" It lay face-up in Marisa's outstretched hand.

All my love always. Rob.

"What do you say to that, Bren? That sounds like a keeper sort of love to me, unless you know something about him that the public doesn't know. Is he a predator? A murderer?"

Bren shook her head. "He's perfect," she murmured.

"And two dozen red roses say he loves you."

Deep breath. "Seems to. I don't know why."

"Because you are beautiful. You are—"

"I'm not beautiful. You are. You're a beauty pageant winner. I'm just a..."

Marisa angled her head. "Just a what, Bren? A child of the one true King? Redeemed? Treasured? Worth dying for?"

"You don't understand."

"I think I do. I think you've built a wall around yourself, maybe for protection. Why not let Jesus tear it down and show you who you really are in Him? Why not let Rob love you? Don't turn your back on the gifts God is giving you, honey. He offers more than eternal life. He offers you a full life here and now. You only need to trust Him and reach for it."

Chapter 16

The sledding party was in full swing when Rob turned into Bren's driveway. At least half a dozen cars parked in a row beside the greenhouse. A bonfire flared closer to the house, with several snowsuit-clad people gathered around. Nearby, Marisa's stepdad offered a cup to a child while her mom ladled another from a large pot on a camp stove.

Children shrieked as they slid down the hill on his left. A tube spun toward him and slammed into the low wall of snow built from plowing the driveway. A few kids tumbled against the barrier, laughing. One turned toward him.

"Rob?"

"Davy!" Rob started toward the boy, but Davy jumped the snowbank and barreled into him. Good thing someone had spread sand on the driveway, or he would have been sent flying with the impact. Rob returned the boy's bear hug. "How are you, buddy?"

Davy tilted his head back, eyes accusing. "Where have you been? I missed you."

Rob's throat clogged. "I missed you, too, buddy. A lot." It was true.

"Why didn't you come?"

"I'm sorry." Rob draped his arm over the boy's shoulder. "But I'm here now. I wanted to see you and your sister."

"And my mom?"

"Yes, I definitely want to see her." The heartrending part was that the feeling was mutual, and she still pushed him away.

"Will you help me make a snowman? I want to make the biggest, tallest one ever."

Rob tugged on his mitts. "That's why I'm here."

"Mommy, Mommy, Mommy!" Lila ran across the top of the hill toward Bren, her hair streaming out from beneath her red stocking cap.

Bren crouched. "What's up, sweetie? Are you having a good time?"

"Guess what! Rob's here. He came."

The smile froze on Bren's face. "That's great." Not so great, really. She certainly hadn't invited him, but then, it wasn't her party. Bob had plowed the snow. Wendy had made the hot cocoa. Jase had built the bonfire. Marisa and

160

Kristen and Kristen's mom had baked cookies and brought treats. Todd and his father-in-law had made sure there was a gift for every child to take home later.

No, it wasn't Bren's party. She just happened to be living on the property and had made sure the house was clean and the washroom nearest the door was well stocked.

"Mommy!" Lila tugged at Bren's hand. "I showed him how to make a snow angel. He never knew. We made a whole choir, and Davy helped, too. Rob said it was the heavenly host singing *Gloria* for baby Jesus."

Against her better judgment, Bren's gaze roved over the figures at the bottom of the hill. Not only was there a row of angels indented in the soft snow beside the highway, but a man and three boys were building a seventh snowman. A choir of angels. An army of snowmen. What would be next?

That Rob.

"I missed him, Mommy. He twirled me around and gave me a whisker rub."

Once Bren had found comfort in Rob's arms. Not twirling so much — although there had been a bit of that — but possessive embraces. Not whisker rubs so much, but the glorious sensation of his lips on hers. Softly sweet at times and, other times, more insistent.

Rob loves me.

And not only that, but he loved Davy and Lila. In protecting herself, was she being fair to the children? He'd begun to fill that fatherly role they both so desperately needed.

Down below, he helped Davy lift a huge snowball on top of another one then the two high-fived each other. Davy and his buddy immediately began rolling another ball, but Rob looked around. Looked up the hill. Probably saw her staring in his direction.

I'm only protecting the kids. They'll be devastated when he gets bored of us.

She'd thought of that too late. They were already devastated. And what, exactly, had given her the impression he'd get bored and move on? He wasn't his grandmother. He'd never flung accusations at her about her wild teen years.

Redeemed in Jesus. Could she really grab onto that, recklessly and completely?

Rob lifted a hand and waved.

She returned the acknowledgment.

He bent, scooped up a handful of snow, and slung it at Davy. Davy turned and pelted him back. In seconds, the boys had ganged up on Rob and the whole group dodged amid the snowmen in a full-scale snowball fight.

"I want to have a snowball fight." Lila started toward the nearest sled.

"You hate when Davy throws snow at you or rubs it on your face."

"But Rob is playing with Davy." Lila dropped tummy-first onto a sled and pushed off.

It had been a long time since Bren had been in a snowball fight, and she wasn't going there today. But somehow, she could understand why Lila was eager to get in the fray. She'd be with Rob, and he'd protect her from the boys.

Bren could be with Rob, too. He'd protect her. Love her. Cherish her. With all her heart, she wished she could be loved that much.

Several more kids joined the snowball fight. Some of those boys packed a hard missile and were recruit-ready for major league baseball. Rob was going to have bruises where some of those slammed him, padded snow pants and all, but he'd only had to caution them once to go gently on the smaller kids like Lila and Charlotte, whose snowballs fell apart in mid-fling.

"Hey, Rob!" Todd strode toward him.

Rob stepped out of the line of fire. "Hey. Now I know why you wanted me to come today. Free babysitting service and battering ram."

Todd grinned. "It looked like you were holding your own." He jerked his chin toward the group of kids, still at it. "Bonding with Davy and Lila?"

"Bonded with them a long time ago." Rob let out a long breath. "I missed them, and it appears they missed me, too."

"Talked to Bren at all?"

Rob shook his head. "She's staying clear of me."

"And you've been steering clear of her, too?"

"Well, yeah. I don't want to get into things in public. With all her friends around."

"You're a good man, Rob Santoro."

"Thanks, but it's no more than any guy would do."

Todd chuckled. "Not so, and you know it. Anyway, there's someone I want you to meet. At least, if you plan to continue working for me for the indefinite future?"

The question was deeper than it first sounded. Would Rob stay in Helena, working for Bren's friend Todd, if things with her were never mended? Was he really, truly, in it for the long haul, no matter what?

A snowball smashed into his shoulder. Rob pivoted, catching Davy's impish grin as the boy ducked behind a snowman. That kid needed some snow rubbed in his face. Moderately gently, of course.

Could Rob be there for Davy, even if he couldn't become his dad? Take the boy backpacking and teach him to be a man?

What if Bren married someone else?

His heart twisted. She loved him. He knew it. She wouldn't spurn his love and get involved with someone else. She needed him, whether she'd admit it or not. The kids had definitely shown him today how much *they* needed him.

Rob turned back to Todd. "I'm not going anywhere, and I enjoy working for you. I'll stick around until you fire me."

Todd smacked him in the shoulder. "Not likely." He jerked his chin toward the bonfire. "Come on."

"New hire?" Rob fell into step beside Todd.

"For Kristen and her parents, not for the agency. But we'll be working closely with her in advertising the pageantry. She's taking over from Marisa now, and will likely stay on for at least a year or two."

He followed Todd around the fire.

"Heather, I'd like you to meet Rob Santoro, my right hand man at the advertising agency. Rob, this is Heather Francis. Heather was a runner-up to Miss Snowflake last year, and she's eager to work with the girls as a coach and mentor."

Rob pulled off his gloves and shook Heather's hand. "Pleased to meet you."

She was very pretty, with dusky blond hair just past her shoulders, the kind of woman he might have once been attracted to. But not since he'd met Bren with her zest for everything.

"Nice to meet you, Rob. Have you worked for Todd long?"

He shook his head. "Just a few months. Before that, I worked at an agency in Billings. Are you from Helena?"

"From Missoula, but after getting my degree, I traveled extensively with Habitat for Humanity for several years. Working for the Mackies part-time will mesh well with what I'm doing for Habitat. I'm looking forward to the challenge, and I've always loved Helena."

"Sounds great."

Todd had turned away and now spoke with Jase. How long did Rob need to engage Heather in conversation before it was polite to move on?

"Tell me about your family, Rob."

"Uh. I'm single." And wished he weren't.

"Oh." She let the word linger slightly as she looked up at him.

Rob backed up a step. No more worrying about the politeness factor. "Single with prospects. It was great to meet you, Heather." The prospects might not be very bright at the moment, but they still existed. Plus, he was committed to seeing them through. Committed to Bren, Davy, and Lila.

He took another step back before turning to see Marisa's mom watching with a small grin. "Hi, Wendy." Hopefully he didn't sound as desperate as he felt.

"Want a hot cocoa?"

"Thanks. Sounds good." He accepted a mug and wrapped both hands around it. "I didn't realize there'd be so many people here."

"Most of them are single moms and their kids who garden here with us. Or with Bren, this year. Marisa helped whenever she could."

"Garden with you?"

Bob pointed at the field covered with snowmen and angels. "Marisa turned that whole area into gardens for young mothers to grow food for their families. Teaches them about nutrition, how to cook. All that stuff."

"That's how we met Bren a few years back," Wendy added. "She and her children were part of the first group. Marisa's idea has made a huge difference in Helena."

"She works hard, too." Bob leaned in. "But Bren maybe works even harder now that she's in charge. Marisa and Wendy had each other to rely on. Bren's been doing it mostly by herself."

Rob was supposed to respond to this… how?

"She does." Wendy nodded. "Hard to find anyone more dedicated. More kind and honest. More deserving."

"You're preaching to the choir."

Bob nudged Wendy. "Told ya. Ever thought of running a market garden, Rob?" He glanced around and lowered his voice. "Me and Wendy, we've been thinking of selling Hiller Farm. I've got land enough for us both, and Marisa doesn't want it. She and Jase have built a house over by the Grizzly Gulch Resort."

"I was holding the option open for Marisa, of course," Wendy wove in. "But we've talked, and she's fine with letting it go."

"But Bren…" They wouldn't turn her out, would they? She'd be crushed.

Wendy set her hand on Rob's arm. "Or we might keep the farm for a few years. Bren is managing it well, but she sure can't afford to buy it, even if we gave her a really good deal. Plus, she's so overworked. I'd hoped to be more of a help this year than I was able to, and Marisa traveled more representing pageantry."

Bob and Wendy were devious. He could see where this was going. "I *have* been thinking about buying a place." The apartment had been fine for just him, but as soon as he'd begun seeing Bren, he'd felt confined in the small space. The farmhouse was much more his style. "Hadn't really considered acreage, though."

"Think on it," Bob advised. "House needs some work, but it's solid. Wendy would give you a fair deal."

"Definitely." Wendy winked at him. "We'd like to see Bren taken care of."

"So would I."

Bob clapped him on the back.

Had Rob really said that? But what did it matter? It was true. He loved Bren and, more than anything, wanted to marry her and shower her with every gift he could for the rest of their lives.

"She's a stubborn one, that Bren." Bob nodded firmly. "A bit prickly at times."

Now that was an understatement. "I've noticed. Things aren't going so well right now. We could use some prayers."

The older couple exchanged a look. "You got 'em, son. Take heart."

After thanking them, Rob turned away and took a sip of the cocoa. His eyes searched for Bren without a conscious thought. There she was, still at the top of the hill, loading little kids onto a long sled.

Should he try to talk to her or not? Maybe his presence had made enough of a statement for one day. Maybe a bit of intrigue would do her good. He slurped the cocoa, set the mug in a bin, and headed for his car.

Chapter 17

eather's really nice. You'll like her."

Didn't much matter what Kristen said. All Bren could think of was how long Rob had stood talking to Heather the other day at the sledding party. Heather was petite. Pretty. Poised. All things Bren was not.

Heather worked for a charity. Bren was the face of charity.

Lila twirled beside Bren. "Heather is bee-yoo-tiful."

Exactly.

Kristen leaned closer. "Rob and Jase will be here, prepping for the final push for marketing the pageant."

Rob would be here. Heather would be here. Why would Bren torment herself?

"I'm going to be an angel and wear the pretty white dress Grandma Mackie gave me. I will sing *Away in a*

Manger. Or maybe an angel song. Which is your favorite angel song, Mommy?"

She didn't want to think about angels. "*Away in a Manger* is a great song for you to sing, and you've been practicing. The angel songs are harder."

Kristen looped her arm through Bren's and towed her into the reception room where some of the girls were already gathered.

Bren pulled back. "I don't think I'll stay."

"I want you to. Please?"

"You can watch me practice my curtsy, Mommy." Lila's blue eyes pleaded with Bren's.

She let out a sigh. "Fine. I'll stay just this once."

"Yay!" Lila ran toward the stage.

"Like a lady, Lila," cautioned Marisa.

"Sorry." Lila continued on at a sedate walk.

Marisa and Heather conferred on the platform and laughed together. The little girls gathered in a circle around them.

Everyone thought Heather was so wonderful. Marisa. Kristen. Lila. Probably Rob. She could tell herself that until she glanced across the back of the reception room where he stood beside Jase, who adjusted his camera on the tripod. Rob wasn't watching Heather. He was watching Bren.

Her heart caught in her throat.

He smiled.

She tried to look away and failed. How she'd missed him. She'd been trying to protect herself from heartache.

Protect the kids. But it was all too late. She'd ensured the heartache. Embraced it. Wallowed in it.

The invitation in Rob's eyes was still there. She'd pushed at him. Snubbed him. Been rude to him, but he still waited. For her.

Rob loved her. She loved him. It wasn't the same thing she'd called love as a teen. That had been physical attraction. Lust. Sure, she longed to taste Rob's kisses again, feel his arms provide a tight, safe cocoon. His caresses had stirred desire, but it wasn't only physical. He offered her more, or he would if she just let him.

Even now he stood not twenty feet away, watching her. The smile had faded a little, but the intensity in his gaze had deepened. He wasn't going to make the first move. She'd pushed hard enough that he'd respect her boundaries.

He'd played with her kids last Saturday then left without a word to her. *Rob this* and *Rob that* was all she'd heard for days afterward. The reproach in her son's eyes had been just as loud as his words. Davy loved Rob. Lila adored him. Rob had proven willing to cherish her kids as his own.

What was she waiting for?

Kristen's elbow nudged her gently. "Go talk to him."

Such a public place. But she couldn't take her eyes off him.

Rob stretched his hand toward her.

Immediately she was back in his parents' kitchen. Rob sat on a stool at the island, his eyes crinkling when she entered the room. He'd held out his hand then, too, and she'd accepted. She'd nestled onto his knee, felt his arms close around her, felt the kisses on her hair.

Loved. Cherished. Protected.

She wanted that again. She wanted that always. Bren took a step toward him, and the smile rekindled, reaching his eyes. She took one more step then another, his warm gaze pulling her forward until she stood just within reach.

Rob grasped her hand and tugged her the rest of the way, sliding his arm around her waist, tight against his side. "I missed you," he whispered, dropping a kiss onto her forehead.

"I missed you, too."

"Away in a manger, no crib for a bed." Lila's sweet soprano trilled across the nearly empty room. "The little Lord Jesus lay down His sweet head. The stars in the bright sky looked down where He lay, the little Lord Jesus asleep on the hay."

Mary had held her baby tightly in her arms. Had nursed him, changed him, and showered him with love, just as Bren had tried to do with Davy and Lila. Mary's neighbors and relatives had thought she'd had sex before marriage, but Joseph had stood with her, believing in her innocence, offering himself as daddy to the Son of God.

Nowadays most people didn't care whether a mom was married or not. How times had changed since Jesus' birth. In fact, His coming had changed everything. He'd come to give her, Bren, hope and a future. To shower her with His love and forgive her sins. If God Himself forgave her, why couldn't she let it go herself?

"Be near me, Lord Jesus. I ask Thee to stay close by me forever and love me I pray," sang her little daughter.

Bren closed her eyes and treasured Rob's arm around her back, his hand rubbing the curve of her hip. *Lord? I'm sorry. I've pushed Your mercy, Your grace, right back at You. I've pushed aside the blessings You've given me. I accept Your forgiveness, Your favor. I know I'm not worthy, but I'm not going to dwell on it anymore. Help me move forward, and thank You.*

A lightness filled her as she slipped her arm around Rob's waist, breathing in the scent she'd missed. New beginnings. She'd trust God. Trust Rob. They'd talk later. For now, this was enough.

He was supposed to be paying attention to the pageantry practice, but he stared at one little girl after another with unremembering eyes. Every cell in his body savored Bren's nearness. Rob wanted nothing more than to wrap her close and kiss her deeply. But, somehow, he needed to do his job. Ideas for ad copy, for an article to submit to the Independent Record. Focus.

The cell phone in his pocket rang. Out of habit, he fumbled for it with his free hand. His mom?

"Hi."

"Rob, please pray for your cousin Dafne. She didn't come home last night, and your Uncle Dino and Aunt Betta are worried sick."

An image of Dafne's face from Thanksgiving entered Rob's mind. "What do they think happened?"

"She's been seeing this boy they don't like, running with a wild bunch."

"Oh, no. I'll pray for sure. If you hear anything, let me know."

"Yes, yes. I will. What of Bren? Have you talked to her yet? You're leaving your mamma in the dark."

Rob's thumb caught in Bren's belt loop. "I'll get back to you on that. I'm working right now."

"But it is Saturday, no? Your day off?"

"Usually. Not today. I'll talk to you later."

"Okay, well, don't forget. You never call."

"I will. Promise." He thumbed the phone off.

Bren looked up at him. "Everything okay?"

He shook his head. "One of my cousins is missing. Whether she's run away or something else happened, no one knows at the moment."

"Oh, no. Who? Was it someone I met?"

"Dafne. Peter's youngest sister."

Bren bit her lip and looked away.

An odd reaction. "Did you meet her? She and the other girls her age were setting tables and doing cleanup."

"I remember her."

What wasn't Bren saying? "Did you talk to her at all?"

"Just to say hello. Nothing more than that."

"I see." Which wasn't precisely true. "Anyway, my mom phoned to ask me to pray for Daf." He hesitated a moment. "Will you pray for her, too?"

Bren nodded, still not meeting his gaze. "Yeah. Definitely."

The little girls clapped, and Rob turned his attention to the rehearsal. For this exact moment, he'd take what he could get, and that was Bren beside him again at long last.

A half hour later, Kristen bustled over. "Bren, the girls have been begging to play together. Do you mind if I take Lila home with me for a few hours?" She looked between the two of them. "I can drop her off later. Whenever you want."

Oh, so subtle. Rob couldn't help winking at his boss's wife.

"I... um, sure. Davy is with friends this afternoon."

"Great. They'll be so excited. Did you get some good shots, Jase?"

Rob had all but forgotten the photographer on the other side of him.

"Yep, some." Jase nestled his camera into its padded case. "I'll send over what I've got later."

"Sounds good." Kristen wiggled her fingers at all of them as she hurried toward the platform.

"Coffee?" Rob turned to Bren. "My place, yours, or the Fire Tower?"

She bit her lip as she glanced up at him. "My place, I think. I don't want to cry in public."

Oh, man. He wrapped both arms around her and pulled her close. "No tears required."

Bren gave a shaky laugh. "I guarantee there will be some."

Rob kissed the top of her head. "I've got one stop to make on my way, but I'll be there soon. Okay?"

"I'll put the coffee on."

"Deal."

Half an hour later, Rob stood on her doorstep with colorful daisies. Bren swallowed the lump in her throat and blinked back the tears. She didn't deserve... no. No more negative self-talk. "They're beautiful." She took them from his hands.

"Not as beautiful as you." Rob dropped a quick kiss to her lips then bent to remove his boots.

She wanted more kisses, but she had to say her piece first. And then, it would be up to him. "Coffee's on. I'll put these in water." Every step away from him tore her soul, but he was here. They'd make things right.

"Bren." At the sink, he wrapped both arms around her from behind, nuzzling into her neck. "I love you so much."

She turned off the faucet and closed her eyes, absorbing the reality of his strong arms. His steadfast love. It took a few seconds for her to think she might be able to keep her voice steady. "Pour us each a coffee?"

He nibbled her ear. "Will do."

A chill ran down her back when he stepped away. The cupboard door opened and closed, then the sound and aroma of pouring coffee. Bren adjusted the flowers in the vase, swallowing the lump in her throat. She waited until he'd seated himself at the kitchen table then took the chair across from him. She lifted her gaze to his. "I'm sorry for everything, Rob."

He nodded, holding her eyes captive.

"You know... you know what my hang-up is. You know that I've always felt defensive about my past. The life I led. The kids. All that."

Rob nodded again.

Well, she'd wanted him to give her room to talk, and he was. She should be thankful. She *was* thankful. "I became a Christian three years ago. Jesus changed me. I can't tell you how much. It was amazing."

He reached across the table and captured her hand.

"But I still didn't feel worthy." She took a long breath. "I think... I think it's not supposed to be about me. About how I feel. It's all about Him, and what He did for me. He's given me gifts that I've refused. I must hurt Him."

His thumb swirled slow circles over the back of her hand.

"I've asked Jesus to forgive me, Rob. I want to embrace His gifts, not sit on the sidelines and just be glad I found salvation. I've been missing a lot." She refocused on his face. "Can you forgive me?"

"I can forgive you. I already have. I want to walk beside you, waiting for God's best gifts for us, but you need to know something, too."

"What?"

"I'm not perfect. I will get angry sometimes. Say something I shouldn't. We may disagree or even argue sometimes. But I will still love you. Do you understand?"

The message was mixed. She couldn't imagine a harsh word from Rob. He'd been so patient with her. Steady like a rock. That he would keep loving her, she could grasp. He'd already been doing it through thick and thin.

Bren nodded. "There's more."

His eyebrows rose. "Go ahead."

"In Spokane. Thanksgiving."

"What happened, sweetheart?"

"I overheard a conversation in the kitchen when I came out of the washroom. It was your grandmother." Man, this was hard. "She was talking to Dafne."

Rob leaned over the table and tightened his grip. "What did she say?"

"To be careful or she'd end up like me." Tears dribbled down Bren's cheeks. "That pierced me. I couldn't handle it. I just couldn't."

"Bren."

She couldn't look at him.

"Sweetheart."

Her heart broke all over again. "What?" she whispered.

"I want Dafne to be just like you."

Bren yanked her hands away. "What on earth are you talking about? Don't you know? Have you already forgotten?"

"I want her to be a woman who loves God, who takes her life, whatever it is, and accepts God's gifts. Who is a devoted friend, a loving mother, a conscientious person who is always helping those around her. You're a child of the one true King, Bren. I want Dafne to be just like you."

Bren stared into the face of the man she loved. He was serious. This was the way he saw her? Not the blemishes, the tarnished halo, the big mess? "You don't know what that means to me." No one had ever told her she was a good role model.

"I love you, sweetheart. With all my heart. As far as I'm concerned, there is no better woman on the planet. Not my mom. Not my grandmother..." He grinned wryly. "Who, yes, has been known to be rather blunt and even rude from time to time but, I promise you, she's on your side, because she's on my side and on God's side." Rob stood and held out his hands.

Slowly Bren rose to her feet, rounded the table, and felt Rob's strong arms enfold her. Then he tipped her face toward his and brushed kisses across her forehead, her cheeks, and her nose before capturing her mouth. A moment later he pulled away, resting his forehead against hers. "I love you, Bren. I'm so glad we're back."

For the first time ever, Bren got the words out in response. "I love you, Rob." She tangled her fingers in his hair, pulled him closer, and kissed him thoroughly.

Chapter 18

Christmas Eve. Rob slid Bren's coat off her shoulders and handed it to the coat checker in the Helena Civic Center lobby. She looked absolutely amazing tonight in a green sheath dress with a sparkly shimmer. Her hair, usually loose, was done in some kind of a knot on top of her head, exposing the neck he would like to kiss. But not now.

He placed one hand to the small of her back and the other on Davy's shoulder. A phone call to his cousin Michael's mom had resulted in a FedEx parcel containing the black suit Michael had worn to a family wedding last spring. It fit Davy to a tee.

As the family of one of the contestants, they were escorted to a table near the front where Todd, Kristen, and Liam already waited. "Nervous?" asked Kristen. "I can't believe I am, after all this."

Bren smiled at her friend as Rob seated her. "A little, yes."

"They'll be fine." Todd stretched his arm across the back of Kristen's chair. "No stress. Remember? A good time for them all."

"I can't believe how good it has been for Lila this fall," Bren said. "Her manners are a thousand times better than they were, and she no longer sounds like a charging elephant everywhere she goes."

Davy snickered.

Bren looked past Rob to her son. "Maybe I should sign you up for deportment classes."

The boy's eyebrows rose. "Deport-what?"

"How to walk. How to handle yourself."

A look of horror crossed Davy's face, and all the adults laughed.

Rob patted the boy's back, and Davy leaned into him. "How to hike. How to cross rivers on a log. How to zoom down a mountain on skis."

"That sounds more like it. Lila walks all prissy now. I don't want to walk like a girl."

One of the other pageant moms stopped to chat with Bren and Kristen on her way to her own table. Then another. The Mackies took their seats near the microphone as chairs around the ballroom filled up. Rob shifted to look toward the ready room door where the girls would soon appear on Marisa's cue. Jase, clad in a black tuxedo, adjusted his camera.

Just as the clock turned five-thirty, Kristen's dad rose and walked to the microphone. "Welcome to the Miss Snowflake Pageant! I'm your host for the evening, Dr. William Mackie."

Immediately the buzz in the large room began to quiet. Bren angled herself toward the platform then glanced over her shoulder at Rob. He shifted closer and rested his hand on her shoulder. She smiled at him, and his heart swelled. Soon he'd ask her to be his forever, but tonight was Lila's night.

"Thank you for coming. We'll start out this evening with the pageant for girls ages seven through ten. Seven young ladies have been preparing for the past two months and are ready to entertain you this evening. Please give a big hand to our Little Misses!"

The room exploded with applause then Dr. Mackie introduced the girls. Each posed for Jase's camera before mounting the steps to the platform, curtsying, and taking her place beside the others. Lila and Charlotte came in the middle, clad in the same navy leggings and tops as the others.

The girls performed a line dance together. Rob could see the judges over at the head table already making notes before the contestants skipped their way offstage.

Dr. Mackie invited someone to lead a Christmas carol. After all the verses to *Joy to the World*, he took the microphone again. "Now the contestants will come, one at a time, and perform their talent. First up, Miss Emily Abercrombie."

The girl performed a tap-dancing routine to Celtic music. The next recited a poem, only stumbling once over her lines. Lila soon came onstage wearing her angel costume, a glittering halo around her blond hair. The words of *Away in a Manger* had never sounded sweeter to

183

Rob's ears. Charlotte followed, playing *Carol of the Bells* on the piano.

When all the girls had performed their pieces, the audience sang another carol while they waited. Soon enough, Emily was back on stage in a pretty dress.

"In this final segment, I have a question for each of the girls." Dr. Mackie turned to the audience. "They know the list of questions, but not which one I'm going to ask of each of them. In fact, I don't even know." He gave a nervous chuckle and held up a top hat, giving it a shake. "The seven questions are in this hat, and I'll draw one for each girl. Miss Emily Abercrombie, here is your question." He unfolded a paper. "What is the hardest thing you've ever done?"

Emily stepped forward, and Heather handed her the mic. "The hardest thing I ever did was climb to the top of the jungle gym at school." She took a few more sentences to describe why that had been so terrifying. Then she posed once more for the camera and took her place off to the side.

Two more girls answered their questions before Lila, wearing a pretty white dress with red ribbons, climbed the steps one last time.

Dr. Mackie pulled out another slip of paper while Marisa handed the mic to Lila. "Miss Lila Haddock, here is your question. If you could have any wish come true, what would it be?"

"I wish every kid in the whole world could have a mommy and a daddy who loved them and have enough food to eat. I wish everyone would get along and be nice to each other and share. And I wish they could know Jesus."

Rob pulled Bren against his chest. "That's awesome," he whispered into her hair. He was going to make part of Lila's wish come true just as soon as he could.

"I can't believe how composed she is," Bren whispered back.

Lila stood with the other girls while Charlotte stepped up wearing a matching dress.

"The next question is for Miss Charlotte O'Brien." Dr. Mackie unfolded a paper. "Who is someone you admire most, and why?"

Kristen squeezed her eyes tight and clenched her hands. Todd chuckled and rubbed his wife's shoulder.

"I admire my auntie Marisa, only she's not my auntie yet for two more weeks until she marries my uncle Jase. I admire her because she is beautiful but also because she is very kind. She plays games with me and taught me how to read books. And she asked me to be her flower girl." Charlotte glanced back at Lila. "And Lila, too. This is my pretty dress for the wedding. See?"

Kristen sagged against Todd.

"They did well," Rob whispered to Bren.

She nodded, her bun brushing his cheek. Did they really have to stay for the Miss Snowflake pageant, too? Why couldn't they sneak out right after dinner and have a cozy Christmas Eve out at the farmhouse? Read a Christmas story, tuck the kids in bed, and enjoy a quiet evening together. He'd return in the morning and see the kids' delight in the gifts he'd chosen for them.

He had something for Bren, too.

"The judges have made their decisions. Contestants for Little Miss Snowflake, are you ready?" Dr. Mackie reached for the papers from the judges' table.

The girls smiled nervously.

"Little Miss Photogenic is Miss Samantha Kujak."

The crowd applauded. Lila and Charlotte clung to each other's hands, holding onto their smiles as the girls around them accepted the congeniality, attire, and talent awards.

Then Dr. Mackie slipped the next piece of paper out of its sleeve. "Second runner-up to Little Miss Snowflake is Miss Lila Haddock. Congratulations, Lila!"

Lila and Charlotte grabbed each other's hands and jumped up and down before Lila stepped forward to accept her trophy and flower. She curtsied and stepped back just as Charlotte was announced the first runner-up. Emily was crowned Little Miss Snowflake a moment later.

Squealing, Kristen squeezed Bren's hands. Like daughters, like mothers. Rob exchanged a grin and a thumbs-up with Todd.

Davy tapped Rob on the shoulder. "She did pretty good, huh?"

"Yeah, she did, buddy. Pretty good indeed."

                  ℰ ☾ ☾

Snowflakes drifted onto Bren's upturned cheeks. The magical pageant was over. Not only had Lila won a trophy, but Marisa had crowned her successor and was officially no longer Miss Snowflake. Bren wrapped an arm around each of her kids as they waited for Rob to bring his car around.

"It's cold, Mom," Lila whined. "My flowers are going to freeze."

"Can I take my tie off *now*?" begged Davy.

He'd only asked about ten times that evening. "No, not until we get home. It's Christmas Eve. Aren't you guys excited?"

"Santa isn't real," Davy announced. "What's to be excited about?"

"It's still Jesus' birthday." Lila peered around Bren. "And we get presents."

"Grandma Mackie has invited us for Christmas dinner tomorrow, too." One of the many events the Mackies loved to host in the resort dining room.

"Yay! I get to play with Charlotte again."

"How come they don't have any boys my age? Liam's just a baby."

"He's not a baby. He's four."

"I'm almost ten. He's a baby to me."

Way past their bedtime. "Kids. Stop. Look, there's Rob's vehicle. Come on."

"Mom! Davy pushed me."

"Did not. I slipped and you were in my way."

Rob came around and opened the back door for Lila then the front one for Bren. As he walked back around, his phone rang. He answered as he slid into the driver's seat.

"The car's still cold, Mom."

"Shh, Lila." Rob said something at the same time, which Bren couldn't catch. "It will warm up in a minute. Rob just started it."

Rob drove around the corner and parked, listening intently to the phone against his ear. "Yes, of course. Where are you? ... Where in Missoula?"

"Can I take off my tie now, Mom?"

She fluttered a hand in irritation. Why couldn't the kids just be quiet, so she could figure out who was calling Rob?

"I can be there in just over two hours. Maybe closer to three, depending on road conditions."

Bren's hopes for a cuddly Christmas Eve evaporated as she shivered.

"No, it's no problem. I'm glad you called. You can stay as long as you need to. Stay safe until I get there, okay?"

He listened for another minute then clicked the phone off. He glanced at Bren. "Dafne."

Annoyance melted. Hope surged. "Is she okay?"

"I think so. I know this isn't how we'd planned the evening, but I need to go get her."

"I understand totally."

"Also, she asked for you. Can you put her up for a few days, maybe? She's my cousin and all, but I don't want a young woman staying with me. I hate to ask."

"Of course she can. But... she asked for me?"

Rob shifted the car into gear and merged with the other cars leaving the Civic Center. "She did. It might have been because of what Nonna said to her at Thanksgiving." He glanced across the car, his hand reaching to squeeze Bren's.

Those hurtful words had turned Bren into a haven instead of an embarrassment? How like God.

"I hate the thought of her in a shelter in Missoula on Christmas Eve." Rob shook his head. "Any time, really. But it will be after midnight before I can reach her. I don't dare wait any longer to leave."

Only a month ago Bren had woken him in the middle of the night and he'd rescued her with just as few questions. How she loved his compassionate heart. "I understand. I do." She looked in the backseat at two pairs of eyes peering back. "Do you two remember meeting Dafne in Spokane?"

They shook their heads.

"You know that when Jesus was born on the very first Christmas, his parents didn't have a house. They had to stay in a borrowed barn."

"With a manger," piped up Lila. "And cows and sheep."

"Right. But what I'm saying is that someone let Mary and Joseph and baby Jesus have a place to sleep, so we're going to do that for Rob's cousin Dafne. Okay? When you wake up tomorrow morning, she'll be at our house, probably sleeping on our sofa."

"Will Santa bring a present for her?"

"I told you. Santa's not real."

"Mom! Davy says—"

Rob chuckled as he turned into their driveway. "There will be a present for Dafne. Don't worry. But the best present she can have is a safe place to sleep, okay?"

"And the best present for your aunt and uncle is knowing she's okay." Bren rested her hand on Rob's thigh.

"Yeah. I need to call them. She didn't want them to know where she was, but it's not fair to them. They've been so stressed out."

He parked the car but left it running as he came around to open doors. The kids scampered inside.

"Pajamas!" called Bren after them before turning to Rob.

He shut the door, closing the blowing snow outside, and gathered her in his arms. "I love you, Bren. Thank you for accepting this curve ball. I'll make it up to you, I promise."

"Drive safely, okay? It's snowing like crazy."

"I'll be fine. The Jeep has good tires, and I've driven in a lot worse conditions." He traced her lips with his finger. "Get some sleep. I'll be waking you up soon enough with Dafne."

"Text me from Missoula?"

"Okay, but you better not be awake to read it." He kissed her gently and pulled back, regret shining in his eyes.

Bren slid her finger between his throat and shirt collar. "You might want to take a few minutes to stop by your place and change. You'll be more comfortable."

He glanced down, looking surprised that he still wore a tuxedo. "Yeah. I'll do that. Merry Christmas Eve." A moment later his vehicle motor quieted as he drove away.

"Mo-oom!" whined Lila.

Bren sighed and turned back to her present reality.

Chapter 19

"ommy, did Santa come?"

Bren groaned and rolled over, pulling her pillow over her head. This was their second Santa-free Christmas, but Lila refused to stop believing.

"I told you. Santa's not real." Davy again.

"But it's Christmas, and I want presents."

Bren could envision Lila's lower lip trembling while tears filled her eyes. Just because Bren had spent an hour awake in the middle of the night getting a withdrawn Dafne settled on the sofa didn't mean it wasn't Christmas morning. The benefit had been sneaking a few hugs and kisses with Rob while Dafne showered. Then he'd left for his apartment, asking her to call when the household was awake.

The man needed his sleep, but he would not be happy if she didn't call.

"What time is it?" she mumbled.

"Six. Five. Nine," announced Lila.

"It's still dark outside." Dafne needed *her* sleep, too. All of them did, but it was later than Bren had dreaded.

"But it's Christmas morning!"

Bren sat and fluffed her pillows. "Come on up, you two."

Lila scampered across the bed and tucked in against Bren, while Davy perched on the edge, watching them both.

"C'mere. You're not too old for a Christmas morning snuggle."

He gave her a lopsided grin and let her draw him close.

"Today is a special Christmas day—" she began.

Lila's head popped up. "Because Rob is coming. Is he going to be our dad?"

"I'm not sure." Her kids deserved more honestly than that. "I hope so, but don't ask him, okay? Let him decide when it's the right time to talk about it, if he wants to."

"Will he bring presents?"

What was with the girl and her need for gifts? "There are presents for both of you under the tree right now from Rob. He left them after you went to bed." At three in the morning, to be more precise.

"Then it's okay if Santa's not real." Lila snuggled back down.

"Jesus is real, and it's His birthday. We give each other gifts to celebrate His birthday."

"That doesn't seem fair," Davy said. "Why don't we give anything to Him?"

194

Bren's heart squeezed. "We do. We give ourselves. We give Him love and praise and thanks."

"Those are funny gifts." Lila peered up.

Bren caressed her daughter's side. "Would you rather have presents, or would you rather have a home and love and friends?"

Silence for a moment.

"Remember what you said at the pageant last night? That you wished every kid could have all that?"

"I'd rather have you," Lila whispered. "But I want Rob, too."

"We're lucky enough to have all those things. And we have a teenager on our sofa who needs us to love her right now. She has a mom and dad who love her, but she was feeling sad and angry and she ran away."

"Why was she sad?"

How much to say? What could a seven-year-old grasp? "We'll talk about that later."

"Mommy? Are there any presents under the tree for her?"

Bren nodded. "Last week I bought myself a pretty top that I really like, but I haven't worn it yet. It looks like Dafne is about my size, so I wrapped it up for her. And Rob brought something, too. I don't know what."

"What can me and Davy give her?"

"I'm not sure, sweetie. You don't have to give her anything except be nice to her."

"But that's not fair."

Bren smoothed Lila's hair. "I know, but we didn't know she was coming until after the stores closed, so we don't have many options."

Lila scooted to the edge of the bed. "I'll find something."

"Me, too." Davy swung his legs over his side.

Wow. She must've done something right, raising these two. *Thank You, Jesus, for their considerate hearts.* "See what you can find. I'm going to have a shower, okay? Stay out of the living room until I say. Dafne didn't get much sleep."

Lila paused at the door. "When is Rob coming?"

"Soon. I'll let him know we're up."

"Okay." She scampered across the hall to her bedroom, her brother behind her.

Bren reached for her cell and touched Rob's number.

"Hey, sweetheart." He sounded beyond exhausted.

"Merry Christmas, honey." Not that she hadn't told him at three in the morning, but still. "The kids are up and asking for you."

"I'll be there in half an hour." He already sounded more awake. "I can't wait to see you."

"I love you, Rob." After getting the words out once, they came more easily, thrilling her every time she said them.

"I love you, Bren. See you soon." But hearing words of tenderness from him was far more thrilling.

Rob sat on Bren's sofa with Lila snuggled on his lap and Davy wedged against his side. Dafne was curled up in an armchair, looking like she was trying to shut them all out. Probably the realities of Christmas morning in a stranger's house had sunk in. Cousin or not, he wasn't much more than a stranger to her, either, at twelve years her elder.

But she'd called him. Because of Bren. She was safe, and he was going to do what he could to reunite her with his parents. Aunt Betta had wept with relief when he'd called last night.

Bren bustled in carrying a tray loaded with hot cocoa, setting one down beside Dafne and three on the coffee table in front of Rob. Not that he could reach his with an arm around each child. He caught Bren's gaze and marveled again at the love shining from her eyes. The wariness was gone. She handed a Bible to Davy, just as they'd discussed a few days ago when they'd planned Christmas morning, though not everything had gone to script.

Davy straightened, opened it to the bookmark, and began reading. "In those days a decree went out from Caesar Augustus that all the world should be registered." The boy stumbled a bit over the difficult names but kept reading. "She gave birth to her firstborn son and wrapped him in swaddling cloths and laid him in a manger, because there was no place for them in the inn."

Lila sat up. "Like in *Away in a Manger*."

Rob kissed the child's hair. "Just like that. Go on, Davy."

"And an angel of the Lord appeared to them, and the glory of the Lord shone around them, and they were filled with great fear."

"Why were they scared?" Lila interrupted. "Angels are pretty and play harps."

"We pretend they are, but the Bible describes them as terrifying. Why don't we let Davy finish reading the story, and we can talk about angels more later?"

"Okay." She leaned back against his chest.

Was he ready to be a dad to another man's children? *Two* other men's children? A thousand times, yes. Those guys had no idea what they'd walked away from. A strong, beautiful woman who'd come to love Jesus. Two bright, happy children capable of just about anything. Rob met Bren's gaze. A slow smile crept across his face. He couldn't help it. He was so, so blessed.

Davy had finished reading and looked up at him expectantly. Rob cleared his throat and closed his eyes, holding the children tight. "Dear Heavenly Father, thank You for sending Your Son as a tiny baby." Would he and Bren ever have a baby? Would she want another? "Thank You that He was — is — perfect, and can save us from our sins. Thank You for second chances, for salvation, and for the gift of eternal life. I thank You for Bren, for Davy, for Lila, and for Dafne, and I pray You will bless our time together today. May we honor You in everything we say and do. In Jesus' name, amen."

Lila straightened. "Is it time for presents now?"

Bren chuckled. "Yes, it is. Do you want to give them out?"

The little girl jumped down and ran to the tree in front of the large window. She grabbed a small, lumpy package, its crooked paper covered with tape, and held it out to Dafne. "Merry Christmas."

Dafne looked from Lila to Bren to Rob. "For me?"

"Looks like it." Rob gave her an encouraging smile.

The teen picked off the tape and revealed a small plastic pony with dirt smudged on its rump. She turned it over with a quizzical look on her face.

Lila clasped her hands behind her back. "She's my favorite. See? She has a rainbow mane and tail. Isn't she pretty?"

Rob watched Bren as she bit her lip, waiting for the response.

Finally, Dafne looked at the little girl. "Thank you. She's very pretty."

"Get another gift," Bren encouraged.

"Here's a big box with my name." Lila stared at in awe.

Rob settled on the floor beside the tree. "Why don't you open it? Davy, here's one for you." He slid a large lumpy package toward the boy.

Both kids ripped into the paper so quickly it made his head spin.

"A backpack! It's awesome." Davy's eyes shone. "Thanks, Rob. Does this mean you're taking me camping?"

"Sure does, buddy."

Davy tackled him with a hug.

Lila squealed. "A cooking set? It's real. Look, Mommy! There's an apron and a mixing bowl and pans and everything."

Bren nestled against Rob on the floor. "I know, sweetie. Rob remembered you like to help in the kitchen."

"Thanks, Rob." The little girl gave him a sloppy kiss on the cheek.

Bren pointed at another package. "Can you take that one to Dafne?"

"Sure." Lila pulled it out and ran across the room. "For you."

Rob took the opportunity to tighten his arm around Bren and nuzzle her hair. "Have I told you today that I love you?"

"A couple of times," she whispered back. "Not nearly enough."

"What did you give Dafne?"

"Shh."

The teen lifted a rust-colored top. "It's pretty. Wow."

"If it doesn't fit, we can exchange it. Or if you'd rather have a different color. Or—"

Rob nudged Bren. "Isn't that the one you bought to wear to Marisa's rehearsal dinner?" he whispered.

"Yes, but I can get something else."

"You make me feel bad I only found a gift card for her. Mom keeps me supplied with those in case I can't afford to buy things for myself."

She chuckled.

"Here, Mommy. This says Bren on it. It's for you."

Rob stilled as Bren accepted the small box.

She gave him a questioning look as she slid her nail behind the tape. A moment later she tipped it open to reveal a pearl necklace with its matching earrings. "Oh, they're gorgeous."

"No more gorgeous than you." He brushed his lips over her ear and whispered. "And no gift cards were used or abused in the purchase of this present."

Bren turned and kissed him, eyes dancing. "Thank you, Rob."

The kids tore into boxes of art supplies from Bren, and Davy presented Dafne with a drawing he'd done of the farm. Rob accepted a handsome watch from Bren. In no time, they were clearing aside wrapping paper.

"I'm hungry, Mommy."

Bren shifted slightly away from Rob. "Of course you are. Drink up some of your cocoa. Did you even see the granola bars on the plate? I'll get breakfast started."

"Granola bars? Yum." Lila dragged her new cooking kit over to the coffee table. "Can I learn to make those?"

"One of these days."

Rob surged to his feet and held out his hand to Bren. "Come on. I'll give you a hand with the Eggs Benedict." They strolled toward the kitchen, arms around each other. Once out of sight, Rob turned and gathered Bren in his arms.

She wrapped her arms around his neck and tugged him closer, reaching for his kiss. "Merry Christmas, Rob Santoro. I love you."

Had he ever had a better Christmas? Not that he could remember.

Chapter 20

On the day after Christmas, Rob took the kids up to Divide for their first skiing lesson, leaving Bren alone with Dafne for the first time since she'd arrived. At least, the first time for more than a minute or two.

"Coffee or tea?" she asked the teen.

"Uh, tea, I guess. Do you have chamomile?"

Five kinds of coffee, for sure, but chamomile? Hadn't Marisa left some in the back of the cupboard? She had. Bren fixed the tea, poured herself a coffee, and set a plate with Christmas cookies on the table.

She eyed the girl. "Rob told me you'd specifically asked for me. We only met one time, but didn't even talk to each other, really. May I ask why you wanted me now?"

Dafne glanced up then refocused on the mug in front of her. "I'm pregnant."

Air whooshed from Bren's lungs, removing the capacity to speak. *Please, Lord, give me words for this hurting child. Guide me.* There were a thousand things she could say wrong right now. Where to even start? What had she needed when she'd taken that pregnancy test and discovered Davy was forming inside her?

"I'm sorry. It's a tough road."

"My boyfriend wanted me to get an abortion. That's why we left Spokane. But I couldn't do it."

Bren nodded. "Abortions can haunt you for the rest of your life. I'm glad you chose not to."

"I won't be seventeen until spring. I can't be a mom."

You should have thought of that before you started having sex. Wrong thing to say. True, but wrong thing. "There's adoption. Lots of couples can't conceive. There are loving homes waiting for a baby."

"How old were you?"

"Same as you. Eleventh grade."

"But you didn't have an abortion and you kept your baby. Why?"

"I was really messed up, Dafne. My dad was long gone. My mom didn't care what happened to me. I had no sisters or brothers. I didn't know Jesus. All I could think of was that I'd created someone who would love me back. No one else did."

Dafne took a sip of tea.

"It's different for you. You have parents and a family who love you." Bren paused. "Do they know?"

Dafne shook her head. "I did some dumb things. Nonna was right. I should've been more careful, but it was already too late. I thought Connor loved me, but he just got mad and hit me when I wouldn't go into the clinic. I ran away from him, too. I was really scared. My parents are going to be so angry. I don't know what to do."

"So you called Rob."

Long hair hid the teen's face. "Two days later."

"Honey, do you know Jesus?"

"Yeah, but... I haven't really talked to Him in a long time."

"He's waiting to hear from you. Remember the story of the prodigal son? The father was waiting with his arms wide. He wanted to forgive his son and shower him with blessings. God is like that."

Dafne shrugged. "I messed up."

Bren reached across the table and covered the girl's hand with her own. "We all do. You know for certain that I did. But you know what? Jesus still loves me. He was still waiting for me. He still wanted to make me a new person in Him. He forgives, Dafne. He forgives everything we've ever done, if we only ask Him. Trust me. I know this better than many people do."

"But..."

"Honey, I accepted salvation and forgiveness from Jesus three years ago, but I hugged one thing close to my chest and wouldn't give it to Him."

Dafne looked up through her hair.

"I clung to my tarnished halo. I sat at the edge of God's reception hall, right by the door, just glad I got in at all, as messed up as I was. People say God forgives and forgets, that all our sin is covered and wiped away. I couldn't see that. If it were really true, then I wouldn't be a single mother with two kids, right? I mean, the sin might be forgiven, but the results were not wiped away."

She replayed the harsh words of Rob's grandmother from a month before. "Please don't misunderstand. I don't regret my children. I love them and will always do everything in my power to care for them. So it's a mixed bag. I wanted my slate to be wiped clean, but I wanted them, too."

"You have nice kids. I can't believe Davy drew me a picture and Lila gave me her favorite pony. I didn't expect anything at all. Not that pretty top or the gift card from Rob. I was just thankful to have a warm place to sleep. You didn't have to give me stuff."

Pieces in Bren's mind began to snap together to form a clear picture. "That's Jesus for you. Remember, all I wanted from Him was to be saved, too. I didn't expect to be showered with blessings. I didn't expect Him to take the blemish my children represent and turn it into something very, very good."

"Like what?" Dafne's face pleaded for an answer she could grasp.

"God allows us to muddle through and choose our own path. When we push Him away, it's harder to hear His still small voice and make good choices. And sometimes we just don't care — for a while, at least."

"Yeah." Dafne sighed.

"You asked for me because you knew I've been where you're at, right?"

The girl nodded.

"And that's my blessing." One of them, anyway.

Dafne frowned. "I don't understand."

"Would you have called Rob if you hadn't known about me?" If her grandmother hadn't held Bren up as a bad example?

"Maybe. Probably not. He's so much older than me. He's my cousin, but I don't really know him."

"But you did know about me, and you're here. I'm so thankful you came, Dafne. Sure, I wish the circumstances were different, and so do you. But the fact that I've walked your road is the reason you came to me. It's why God brought you here. He's allowing me to bless you. Does that make sense?"

"Yeah, kinda. Mom always says God works things out for our own good." Dafne grimaced. "Not sure how He's gonna work this one out."

"Have you asked Him?" Bren asked gently. "He's waiting for you to ask His forgiveness. He wants you back, not at the edges of His great reception hall, but in the midst of the throng, praising Him for His blessing and mercy."

"I want that," murmured Dafne. "I really do."

"I'm so proud of you." Rob glanced across the car at Bren. His beloved.

Dafne had cried with her parents over Skype last night, and her big brother, Peter, had driven out to meet them in Missoula and take Dafne home. They'd just parted ways.

"I finally got what you said that day, about Romans eight twenty-eight. I even found myself quoting it to Dafne."

"What's ahead for her?"

"She'll have to decide if she's keeping the baby or giving it up for adoption."

"What would you advise?"

"It's so hard to know. My life would have been easier if I'd let Davy and Lila be adopted. I might have finished school and gone to college. I might have some swanky city job."

Hard to imagine Bren in an office somewhere. Rob grinned. "Regret it?"

She shook her head. "Not for a minute. I needed them to get my life turned around. Without them, I'm not sure when or how God would have gotten my attention." She reached across the console and rested her hand on his thigh. "Dafne's lucky. She already knows Jesus and is well on her way to getting back on track. Her parents will be right there with her, helping her."

Bren had been on her own. But not anymore. Not if he could help it. Not if she'd let him.

Today was the day. He'd suggested they leave the kids with Todd and Kristen rather than subject them to five or six hours in the vehicle, and Bren had agreed. Kristen had sweetened the deal, promising to dig out the resort's snowshoes so Davy could clomp around out in the snow since it was a clear, sunny day.

Rob was in no hurry to get back to Helena. He watched for a rest area he'd noticed along the Clark Fork River. There it was. He signaled and turned in.

Bren looked around. "What's up?"

"It's been so busy lately with the pageant and then Dafne and Christmas, it seems I've hardly had five seconds alone with you." Rob parked. "Let's go for a walk."

"I'd like that."

He came around and opened the door for her then beeped the SUV locked.

"I love the crisp air." Bren twirled in the parking lot.

He caught her and held her close. "Me, too. It's nice to clear the lungs." He kissed her nose and pulled away before she could close the gap between their mouths.

Bren's eyebrows rose. "For a guy who wanted to be alone..."

"A parking lot with semis zipping by on the interstate isn't exactly what I had in mind. There's a trail." He caught her hand and tugged her along with him.

A few minutes later they'd crested the rise and come out above the river. The sun glinted off the meager remaining snow.

"How was Christmas for you?" Rob glanced at Bren and swung her hand. "Did you get everything you hoped for?" He could barely keep his face straight.

She narrowed her gaze at him. "I couldn't have asked for a nicer Christmas, other than sleep on Christmas Eve, but that was totally worth losing."

"You weren't hoping for anything more?"

"I... um..."

"I thought of buying you a new set of pots. I saw a great sale on Le Creuset, but they were out. You know, those porcelain-coated cast-iron saucepans?"

"Those are very nice. Very expensive."

"When's your birthday? Maybe I can get them for you then."

"May twelfth." The confusion in her eyes hadn't dissipated.

"I thought of a lot of things to get you, actually. You're fun to buy gifts for."

"The necklace and earrings are gorgeous. I don't need more."

"Nothing?"

She stopped and put both hands on her hips. "Where are you going with this, Rob Santoro?"

He held her gaze as he reached into his pocket and dropped to one knee in the middle of the path. "Will you marry me, Bren?" He popped the velvet box open and held it up for her inspection.

Her eyes widened as she looked from his face to the diamond solitaire and back to his face. "Rob. Are you for real?"

"I've never been more serious in my life. I want nothing more than to spend the rest of my life with you, showering you with flowers and gifts and good Italian pasta. I want to wake up beside you every morning, starting each day with a kiss and a prayer. I want to be a real daddy to Davy and Lila. Bren, I want *you*. Will you marry me?"

She pressed her hand to her heart. She'd never been more beautiful, her face glowing in the winter sun, her eyes alive with life and love. "I'm so honored, Rob. I would love to marry you."

Rob slid the ring onto her finger then rose and gathered her close, kissing her like a drowning man seeking a life preserver. "Bren, I love you so much. So very, very much. How soon can we get married?"

"I signed a contract to manage the farm again this year."

They'd talk about buying it later. He had numbers from Wendy. Very fair numbers. "So let's have a wedding before it gets busy. When's that?"

Her eyes shone. "We're planting in the greenhouse in early March."

"February sounds good. You don't need longer than that to plan a wedding, do you? How big does it need to be? How many guests?"

"I've got no one to invite, but you've got an entire clan." She grimaced. "Your grandmother—"

"Nonna will love you. I promise. Now I can honestly be thankful for what she said in your hearing. It sent Dafne to you when she desperately needed someone to set her on the right path. Nonna is just as thankful as Uncle Dino, Aunt Betta, Peter..."

She kissed him. "Don't start naming them all. We'll be here until midnight."

"I love you, Bren. Seriously. February? Can we do that? I don't want to wait a minute longer than I have to."

"I happen to be close friends with an event planner or two. I'm pretty sure we can pull it off. I can't believe this."

"Believe it." He closed his mouth over hers and poured all his conviction into his kiss.

Epilogue

B ut you said we'd go backpacking for my birthday. School's out." Davy slumped to the top step in the farmhouse and stared down at Rob.

"We will. We're leaving tomorrow instead."

"But..."

Rob grinned up at him. "Hey, buddy, have I ever broken a promise to you yet? I'm not starting now."

"It sounds like it."

Bren appeared in the kitchen doorway, out of Davy's line of sight. She raised her eyebrows, obviously questioning if she needed to set the boy straight. Rob drank in the sight of his precious wife as he shook his head slightly. If they had extra time before the appointment, he'd spend it kissing her. He gave her a rueful grin, and a soft smile spread across her face.

213

Lila skipped up behind Davy, twirling in her new summer dress. She'd grown so much in the past few months she no longer fit either of her flower girl dresses, to her dismay. Rob didn't mind buying his princess a new one. *His* princess.

"I'm ready for Davy's birthday party, Rob." She clattered down the steps and launched into his arms from the third one up.

"Oomph." He caught her and swung her around. He'd never be the one to tell her she was too big. He'd soak up the arms tight around his neck and the little girl burrowed her face against his as long as he could. "Come on, Davy. Look. I'm dressed up, too. See, even a tie."

Lila giggled and flipped the end of it as he slid her to the floor.

"I don't want a dress-up party," the boy grumbled. But at least he levered off the step and shuffled to his room.

"I do! I love parties." Lila ran to Bren for a hug.

I do. Words he and Bren had said to each other four short months ago. Words he'd gladly repeat every morning as long as he lived. He crossed the space and wrapped his arms around his wife, with Lila squeezed between them, giggling. "I love you, Mrs. Santoro."

"Back atcha, Mr. Santoro."

"I want to be Santoro, too."

Bren's eyes danced at Lila's words. She stretched over her daughter's head to kiss Rob. "Are we going to be late?"

"Nah, we should be good. Davy's using up all the extra time, though."

"If he only knew."

"Who's going to be at Davy's party? Why are we all dressed up?" begged Lila.

"If I told you, it wouldn't be a surprise."

Lila spun free. "I like surprises."

"Out to the car, sweetie. Let me move your brother along." Bren headed for the stairs, but Davy was on his way down, his shirt untucked and buttons askew. "Here, buddy. Let me comb your hair." She fussed with his hair while Rob straightened the buttons. "Now out to the car. Let's go."

Davy ambled out in no hurry, and they were on their way. A few minutes later Rob parked beside the courthouse, pleased to note the abundance of familiar Washington license plates on the surrounding vehicles.

The boy made no effort to open his door when Rob came around for Bren. "This isn't Grizzly Gulch Resort at all."

"Good observation. We have an errand here, first."

Lila clasped Bren's hand. "Where are we?"

"You'll see. Come on, Davy. Be a good sport."

Rob wrapped one arm around Bren and set his other hand on Davy's shoulder as the four of them made their way into the building.

"Santoro?" asked the receptionist. "Just down the hall. The judge is waiting."

Davy angled a look up at Rob from narrowed dark eyes.

Rob winked back.

The large room was wreathed in darkness except for a light shining over the desk at the front. The judge stood,

215

but the clerk remained seated. "Roberto Santoro? Bren Santoro?"

"Yes." Rob nudged the children forward. "I'd like you to meet David Glen Haddock and Lila Marie Haddock." For the very last time.

The judge bent to the children. "This man wants to be your father. He wants to adopt you, and give you his name." He accepted a paper from the clerk beside him. "When I sign this, your name will be David Santoro. And you will be Lila Santoro."

"Rob!" squealed Lila, jumping at him. "You will be my daddy?"

He caught her. "If you'll be my daughter."

She smooched him. "Yes, please."

Rob crouched, settling Lila on his knee as he looked at Davy. "What do you say? Will you be my son?"

Davy glanced at his mom then the judge then back at Rob. "For real? I can call you Dad?"

"For real. For always."

Davy nodded and grinned, leaning against him. "Yeah, I'd like that. A lot."

Rob's heart was full. "Let's sign those papers then."

He scrawled his name, and so did Bren. The judge and the clerk added their signatures. Then the lights came on in the sitting area, and a huge cheer went up.

"Congratulations to the Santoro family," the judge said.

Probably no one but Rob heard him amid the clapping and whistling that came from their friends and family, at least as many people as had attended the wedding a few months earlier.

If only Rob had three arms to hold his wife and both his children at the same time. He pulled them as close as he could while camera flashes lit the air. Jase wasn't the only one documenting the event.

He stretched across Lila to kiss Bren's cheek. "We have an announcement."

"We heard it, man," hollered his cousin Peter.

"We may be a family of four today, but next winter we'll be a family of five." He looked between Lila and Davy. "You're going to have a baby brother or sister."

"Dibs brother," Davy hollered.

Lila pouted. "Sister, please."

Everyone laughed. Rob squeezed the kids and glanced at his glowing wife. "That's up to God. We don't get to know just yet."

"Congrats!" the chorus welled.

"Everyone's invited to the Gotcha Party out at the resort!" Kristen called.

"Michael's here. Did you see?" Rob asked his son. *His son.*

Davy's face lit up.

"Know what else? He and Peter are coming backpacking with you and me. We're leaving in the morning. Isn't that even better?"

"Yeah. But... are you really my dad now? Because that's pretty awesome."

"Really truly."

Davy messed up Rob's hair with a cheeky grin then ran off to find Michael. Lila squirmed away to show off her pretty dress to Charlotte and Tieri.

For one brief moment in the midst of the chaos, Rob and Bren stood in their own world. She stepped into his embrace, looping her arms around his neck. He could barely feel the tiny bulge pressing against him, but new life had already been planted. He kissed his wife, cradling her close.

"Thank you, Rob," she whispered, gazing into his eyes. "This means the world to me."

"To me, too. I love you."

"I finally have more great grandchildren," came Nonna's voice. "Now, who will be next? Pietro? Jasmine?"

"Hey, don't rush me," Peter joked.

"*Rush* you? You are twenty-six years old, no? See how happy it makes Roberto to have a family. Bren, she is a good woman. There is one for you, too. Settle down already."

Grinning, Rob put both hands in Bren's hair and gave a little twist.

"What was that for?"

"Straightening your halo. It seems to be intact. Not that Nonna could make it any more polished than Jesus did."

"Oh, you." And she kissed him.

Dear Reader

Do you share my passion for locally grown real food? No, I'm not as fanatical or fixated as many of the characters I write about, but gardening, cooking, and food processing comprise a large part of my non-writing life.

Whether you're new to the concept or a long-time advocate, I invite you to my website and blog at www.valeriecomer.com to explore God's thoughts on the junction of food and faith.

Please sign up for my monthly newsletter while you're there! I have a gift for all subscribers there. Joining my list is the best way to keep tabs on my food/farm life as well as contests, cover reveals, deals, and news about upcoming books. I welcome you!

Enjoy this Book?

Please leave a review at any online retailer or reader site. Letting other readers know what you think about *Other Than a Halo: A Christmas in Montana Romance* helps them make a decision and means a lot to me. Thank you!

Better Than a Crown, the third book in the Christmas in Montana Romances, is Heather's story. It's expected to release fall 2017.

If you haven't read my other books, may I recommend the six-book Farm Fresh Romance? The first story is *Raspberries and Vinegar*.

Author Biography

Valerie Comer lives where food meets faith in her real life, her fiction, and on her blog and website. She and her husband of over 35 years farm, garden, and keep bees on a small farm in Western Canada, where they grow and preserve much of their own food.

Valerie has always been interested in real food from scratch, but her conviction has increased dramatically since God blessed her with three delightful granddaughters. In this world of rampant disease and pollution, she is compelled to do what she can to make these little girls' lives the best she can. She helps supply healthy food — local food, organic food, seasonal food — to grow strong bodies and minds.

Valerie is a *USA Today* bestselling author and a two-time Word Award winner. She has been called "a stellar storyteller" as she injects experience laced with humor into her green clean romances.

To find out more, visit her website at www.valeriecomer.com, where you can read her blog, explore her many links, and sign up for her email newsletter to download the free short story: *Peppermint Kisses: A (short) Farm Fresh Romance 2.5*. You can also use this QR code to access the newsletter sign-up.

Made in the USA
Monee, IL
10 June 2021